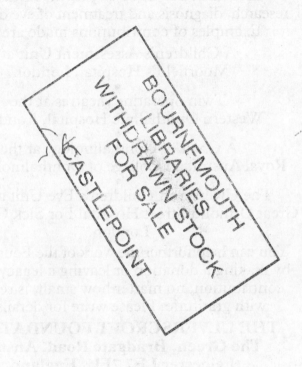

UNDER A SINGLE STAR

Roscoe Byrnes was a carefree playboy until, on the orders of his father, an officer in the Confederate States Army, he was obliged to take up arms. He proves to be a fine and courageous soldier, but events shatter all his hopes and disaster strikes when he discovers that his best friend is an officer in the opposing army. However, with the Civil War at its height and horror and bloodshed surrounding him, Roscoe must battle on — or die.

Books by T. M. Dolan
in the Linford Western Library:

GUNS OF THE PONY EXPRESS
AIM BEFORE YOU DRAW
WEST OF ASH HOLLOW

T. M. DOLAN

UNDER A SINGLE STAR

Complete and Unabridged

LINFORD
Leicester

First published in Great Britain in 1999 by
Robert Hale Limited
London

First Linford Edition
published 2000
by arrangement with
Robert Hale Limited
London

British Library CIP Data

Dolan, T. M.
    Under a single star.—Large print ed.—
Linford western library
    1. Western stories
    2. Large type books
    I. Title
823.9'14 [F]

ISBN 0–7089–5714–5

Published by
F. A. Thorpe (Publishing)
Anstey, Leicestershire

Set by Words & Graphics Ltd.
Anstey, Leicestershire
Printed and bound in Great Britain by
T. J. International Ltd., Padstow, Cornwall

This book is printed on acid-free paper

Author's Note

On 20 December, 1860, South Carolina seceded from the Union on the ground that it was a league of states, and not a nation. At 4.30 a.m. on 12 April, 1861, a 10-inch mortar at Fort Johnson belched smoke, flame — and a round shell exploded over Fort Sumter. That shell began the American Civil War that was to last four years. Fort Sumter was manned by Union States of American troops, while raised over the Confederate States of America's Fort Johnson was a red flag with a palmetto tree and a crouching tiger. 'A single star completes the symbolism,' the South Caroline *Daily Courier* reported at the time.

T.M.D.

1

Situated on sinful Sixth Avenue, the Bowery Bastille was proof that New York never slept. The lamplighter had gone his rounds and a great city had become a jungle. It was after midnight now, and the orchestra was playing the quadrille. On an open space at the head of the stairs, where the floor was nicely waxed, dancers glided through the figures with a genuine grace. The girls danced well, laughing to captivate their partners, which was all part of their business. Yet their laughter was devoid of the healthy ring of innocence, and had a hollow cadence. On a nearby platform were round tables at which sat drinking and eating parties. Beer was the most fashionable tipple, and the tables were all wet with it. Waitresses were constantly dashing about filling orders, up to twenty glasses in their grasp. Among their number were a few simpering males who were painted to resemble women and were dressed in female clothes. Only recently tolerated by the public, these 'queers', as they were known, spoke in falsetto voices, eager to exchange raunchy banter with each other and the patrons. The proprietress had taken a chance in employing their moral deformity as an attraction. All of this was seen as good fun, and the atmosphere was pleasant. To make sure it stayed that way, a choice gang of cut-throats and manhandlers were stationed strategically about.

Fifty or sixty young women were in the room. Many of them were intoxicated, several very much so. Behind a long bar, pyramids of fancifully arranged tumblers glittered in the gaslights. On a stage at the far end of the large room, some vulgar statues revolved with all their offensive detail illuminated by limelight. The air was bluish with smoke from cigarettes in which men and women both indulged. There was a standing joke that the Bowery Bastile was so smoky 'that frequently a gentleman has to kiss a dozen ladies before he discovers by the taste which is his wife'.

There was bawdiness here that was made all the more potent by a flimsy veil of decorum. Where the conversation was not low and vile it was flash and cheap. The entertainment was non-stop. Although the free-and-easy quadrille was still in progress there was a card up announcing that a schottische was the next dance. There was no apparent drunkenness, loud conversation, or disorderly conduct. Represented here were all of a great city's immoralities, foibles, frailties, depravities and oppressions. Cait Mackeever liked to brag that no one had met their death in her place. It was something of an idle claim because she was among the many who'd had a narrow squeak.

On the balcony, in a small compartment partitioned off by musty curtains,

Roscoe Byrnes, a fairhaired, handsome, dissipated-looking fellow, sat sprawlingly in partial drunkenness. The surroundings held an undeniable charm for Byrnes, an empty-headed young man with all the self-regard and arrogance of those born into wealth. He was a veteran at 'hunting the elephant', the current common phrase for slumming. Most who knew him had become bored by his oft-repeated boast that though he may not have travelled extensively, he managed to see a lot of the world in one night, every night.

His close companion, Kit Geogheghan, was a stocky, muscular individual. Their long friendship had something of the attraction of opposites to it, for Geogheghan was a self-made man who had struggled for a living all of his life. Lacking Byrnes's looks, elegance and impeccable poise, Geogheghan was the one now surrounded by girls with cheeks bright with excitement and paint. They sidled down beside him like birds going to roost.

As a waiter passed along the balcony, one of the girls asked pleadingly and slurringly, 'Are you going to treat us again, Kit? We've only got ten minutes before we go on in the next dance.'

Their only advances to Byrnes were remote, no more than covert glances. He was desirable for his good looks and considerable wealth, but they knew that he was spoken for. Roscoe Byrnes, New York's most handsome and richest man — discounting Owney Byrnes, his business tycoon grandfather — was the property of Cait Mackeever, who, as owner of the Bowery Bastille, was their boss.

'What are you having?' Geogheghan asked the girls.

'Brandy mash,' replied the one who had made the request, while the others ordered beer.

Before Geogheghan could call the waiter, Cait Mackeever's voice could be heard outside. She ordered her employee to hurry downstairs where he was needed. Business was brisk.

5

The club owner then came in through the curtains, adoration in her eyes as she gazed at Byrnes. Once a beautiful blonde, her beauty was now a shadow cast behind by that which had gone. Yet, despite too little shine in her eyes, and too much rouge upon her cheeks and too much powder shading it, she was still an exciting woman. Cait was wearing a black silk dress, over which a long gold chain trailed like a yellow serpent. The girls who had been caressing Geogheghan rushed out of the compartment.

Standing, swaying precariously at first, a smiling Roscoe Byrnes took a cigar case from a pocket of his blue-coloured suit of fashionably matching waistcoat and trousers. Bowing his head for her to place a kiss of greeting on his cheek, he straightened up to put the cigar between his even white teeth and light it.

'This is a remarkably lively evening, my dearest Cait,' Byrnes said through a cloud of new smoke, 'but you, generous, fair lady, have come to take this condemned man from his miserably lonely cell and lead him to your boudoir.'

'It's a little early for that, Ross,' she answered, rewarding him by laughing at his flowery vocabulary. 'I've just come to make sure that no woman has stolen from me the man I love.'

Byrnes knew why she was there. Like him she wanted time to pass until business slowed and they could be together. A time when the number of customers had dwindled and in the intimacy of the green room he would enjoy the exquisite pleasure of her sitting on his knee sipping champagne. From there they could keep an eye on the bartenders as they poured beer for the last, sleepy-eyed drinkers.

'No one could lure away the man who each night whispers magic to you in your dreams. The man who one day soon will take you for his wife and endow you with all his worldly goods,' he assured her gallantly.

Turning to Geogheghan, a twinkle in her eye, she asked, 'Would you believe this rogue if you were I, Kit?'

'I know nothing of either love or worldly goods,' the black-haired Geogheghan shrugged. 'I am a hard-working butcher. In a few hours' time I will be slaving away yet again.'

The orchestra striking up the merry measures of Offenbach's can-can music prevented Cait Mackeever from continuing the repartee. Lips tightening in anger, producing fine lines around her mouth, she said, 'I left strict instructions for that not to be played. This means trouble, boys. This will bring the law officers, clothed in blue and brass, out from the Merton Street station-house.'

Not caring about the police, but relishing some bawdy entertainment, Byrnes and Geogheghan wore the silly smiles of intoxication on their faces as they swayed from side to side to the beat of the music.

Then the sedate, good behaviour of

the Bowery Bastille clientele took a swift turn for the worst. In a rush of skirts, a troupe of girls came prancing out on a stage at the end of the dance floor. The scene was lent glamour by artfully positioned gaslights. Their lively feet keeping time to the melody in all its lewd suggestiveness, they abandoned themselves to the dance. As the wild gyrations put limbs clad in pink stockings on show, so did the excited audience, shouting encouragement, lose its inhibitions.

Hurriedly leaving Byrnes and the others, Cait dashed along the balcony and held up her skirts to run down the stairs. But she was too late to prevent the catastrophe she knew was looming. The girls had come down from the stage to leap up on to tables. Sad havoc was made of glassware as can-canners danced on every table. Men lowered themselves in their chairs to look upwards for a better view. Others abandoned all pretence by kneeling on the floor. Soon the scene surrounding the wildly dancing girls degenerated into an orgy.

Then things turned nasty. Suddenly there was a crash as a table was upset; one man had struck another in a quarrel about a woman. Soon there were more fights in progress. There was much swearing and the harsh, threatening sound of breaking glass. Women started to scream shrilly, and the lights were turned out. The Bowery Bastille's manhandlers rushed in in an attempt to secure the doors. But it was too late. The doors were forced open and the clatter of heavy boots somehow silenced the riotous revellers so that Cait Mackeever's voice could be heard calling for the lighting to be restored.

When the lights went up there was a concerted gasp of horror from the crowd. Police Captain Silver, stern of face and threatening in his authority, stood, moving his head slowly, as his steely eyes took in the scene. Behind him, drawn up across the entire length of the building, were double ranks of Fifteenth Precinct men.

At once there arose a hubbub, in which women cried out in distress at the shame of being caught in such a place. Some men cursed, while others made a joke of the situation. Everyone glanced frantically around for a means of escape, but the experienced Captain Silver had every exit well guarded.

The girls, their face paint smudged by tears and sweat, were rounded up like cattle. There were more than sixty of them, and the police divided them up so that they could be taken off in relays to the station-house. Some of the brazen ones laughed and spat obscenities at the police officers; others, who came from decent homes and shouldn't have been at the Bowery Bastille, sobbed as though their hearts were breaking.

Cait Mackeever was behind her bar, and Captain Silver strode over to notify her to close down the bar and regard herself as under arrest.

11

'Hold it right there, Captain!'

It was Roscoe Byrnes who had shouted. On the balcony directly above Cait and Silver, with Kit Geogheghan at his side, he stood precariously, holding the drapes with one hand as he pointed a finger at the police captain, saying, 'That woman tried to stop this reprehensible behaviour, Captain. You have no reason to arrest the lady.'

An indignant Silver shouted back, 'You are under arrest with the others, sir, and I would ask you to stay quiet and permit me to carry out my duties.'

'Your duties are on the streets,' Byrnes contradicted him. 'You and your minions are intruders here, Captain.'

'You are drunk. Come down from there before you injure yourself and others,' the captain ordered.

'It is abundantly clear,' Byrnes said in his educated tones, 'that you have no idea to whom you are speaking.'

'I know who you are, young Byrnes,' Captain Silver replied with a short, derisive laugh, 'and I know what you are. A drunken waster, a privileged piece of scum.'

'You would be well advised to watch your mouth, Captain Silver,' an angry Byrnes called.

'My advice is that you shut yours, sir,' Silver answered, signalling two of his men to take Cait Mackeever into custody.

Launching himself from the balcony, the swash-buckling Roscoe Byrnes dropped from a considerable height to land feet first on a table. People scattered as the table collapsed under Byrnes. Drunk though he was, he followed the direction of his fall to go into a roll and come up on his feet facing the police captain.

Not allowing Byrnes the chance of remonstrating, two burly policemen grabbed an arm each so that he was unable to move. Loyalty to his friend from boyhood days made Geogheghan jump from the balcony in support of Byrnes. But he landed badly on a chair

13

that shattered under him. A long piece of jagged wood slashed his head open as he pitched heavily to the floor. Swiftly dragged to his feet by police officers, Geogheghan bled profusely from a long gash in his forehead.

Word of the raid had spread and a throng of curious onlookers pressed forward when they were taken outside. It was a massive operation involving several hundred prisoners. Roscoe Byrnes and Geogheghan were lined up with the other males as arrangements were made to link each pair of arrested men to a policeman.

A line of cabs, their lamps lit, waited for fares that would not now materialize. The shocked driver of the Byrnes family carriage moved it forwards, the wheels rattling over the cobblestones as he called in alarm, 'Mr Roscoe, sir.'

'Wait for me, Peters, I will not be long,' Byrnes shouted to his driver, as a giant of a policeman took charge of him and the still bleeding Kit Geogheghan.

Hearing this, Captain Silver marched up to stop in front of Byrnes, his face stern as he said, 'Send the poor fellow home, Byrnes. You won't be needing him for many a long night.'

'You are a fool, Captain,' Byrnes grinned confidently at Silver. 'Within a short time my grandfather will have learned of this, and you will be ordered to set me free.'

'Not this time.' The captain dismissed Byrnes's words with a shake of his head. 'You and your like have had your last glimpse of Gotham. The Excise Commission will be revoking the licences of these places. Even Owney Byrnes's money won't be able to buy your freedom this time. You are destined for a long stay on Blackwell's Island, Roscoe Byrnes.'

Taking a silk handkerchief from his pocket, Byrnes used it in an attempt to staunch the flow of blood from Geogheghan's forehead. The women were already on the move, and he saw Cait Mackeever's eyes seeking his.

They locked glances. A long silent message that warmed him although he couldn't define it, passed between them until a policeman pushed her roughly and she was taken from his sight.

'This is bad, Ross,' Geogheghan was whispering, holding Byrnes's handkerchief as a pad against his wound. 'I'm going to make a break for it.'

'No, Kit,' Byrnes hissed. 'Stick with me and grandfather Owney will get us both out.'

'Like the captain said, Ross, not this time. They mean business. You and me will end up on the island. Are you coming with me?'

'No,' Byrnes replied, 'but I'll find a way to keep this big oaf occupied while you get away.'

'Thanks, Ross, you're a true friend.'

'Just as you are, Kit. Good luck to you,' Byrnes said, as they shook hands.

'Cut out the talking and get moving,' their captor ordered gruffly.

The long line of prisoners moved off. Only a few of them were ruffians. In the main it was businessmen and workers holding good positions in the city. They had been out for a good time, but were now quaking in their shoes.

Shuffling like slaves heading for a market, the procession of prisoners passed the peculiarly shaped Negro dwelling known as the Coffin House. On Houston Street, they neared the sombre convent of the Sisters of Mercy. Despite the late hour, grey and white-robed nuns did a slow parade on the beautifully kept lawn, intoning prayers, oblivious to the wickedness without.

On reaching the gate to which a box for donations was affixed, Byrnes reached into his pocket with his free hand.

'Cut that out, keep moving,' the policeman ordered.

Pulling out a handful of dollar bills and loose change, Byrnes pleaded, 'Let me make a donation, Officer, to atone

17

for what I have done this night.'

The giant policeman, an Irish Catholic, hesitated. He was off guard enough for Byrnes to drag him towards the gate. As he stretched a handful of money to the box, so did Geogheghan make his move. He somehow broke free, but the policeman reached out a hand to grip Geogheghan's collar with fingers that resembled a bunch of bananas.

Instantly grasping the situation, Byrnes let the money drop into the box while at the same time back-heeling the policeman in the shins. With a grunt of pain, the officer reached down to his injured leg, releasing Geogheghan who ran off in the direction of the Bowery. Watching his friend go, Byrnes was filled with an immense sense of loss. It was a continuation of the wrench he had felt a short time ago when Cait had been taken from him. He couldn't remember a time when the faithful Kit hadn't been at his side.

There was some shouting and yelling, with a few policemen running after the escapee for short distances. But one man mattered little when they still held hundreds captive. As the procession moved on, the policeman he had kicked cuffed Byrnes in the head. The blow was stunning, but a small price to pay for helping his good friend to get free.

Resources at the Merton Street station-house were stretched to breaking point when the parade of former revellers arrived. The prisoners were squeezed in, and officers took names. There was a host of Smiths and Joneses, and an array of distinguished names of men too well known to try concealing their identity. Roscoe Byrnes was part way through giving his details to a policeman when Captain Silver approached.

'Come through to the back with me, Byrnes,' Silver said tersely. 'There's someone to see you.'

'Sent by my granddaddy, I'd wager,'

a relieved Byrnes grinned at the captain.'

'Not exactly,' Captain Silver answered, as he pushed Byrnes into a cell.

The captain stayed outside, shutting the door. Byrnes found himself facing three men. The one nearest to him was tall, stooped, and cadaverously lean; the others were thickset and thuggish.

'Roscoe Byrnes?' the tall man enquired, in a way that said he already knew the answer to his question.

'That's me.'

'I'm Lieutenant Slater of the Confederate States Army.'

Byrnes looked the tall, thin man over insultingly.

'You don't look like much of an army officer to me.'

'In return,' Slater rejoined, with a scathing look at Byrnes's showy but expensive clothes and overlong fair hair, 'I must say that you don't look much of a man to me.'

'I wouldn't say that you and me are likely to get on, Slater,' Byrnes said, turning to bang a fist on the door and shout, 'Let me out of here, Captain Silver.'

'I can't let you go. I am under military orders,' Slater said.

'Whose orders?' Byrnes scoffed, certain now that there had been some kind of mix-up.

'Major Rutherford Byrnes.'

Shock, combined with the alcohol he had consumed, sent Roscoe Byrnes's head reeling. Until that moment his father had been no more than a vague memory. He had been eight years old the last time he had seen him, and couldn't even remember what he looked like. When his wife had died giving birth to Roscoe, Rutherford Byrnes, a restless adventurer, had left the baby for his parents to raise. If his father ever contacted Owney Byrnes, then his grandfather had never mentioned it to Roscoe.

'What's this all about, Slater?' he asked hoarsely.

'Lieutenant Slater,' the tall man

admonished him. 'God knows why, son, but Major Byrnes wants you to serve in our army. Confederate territory is being extended westward to the Pacific coast. My orders are to escort you to Texas, where, heaven forbid, the intention is to swear you in as an officer.'

'Don't get yourself all riled up about it, Lieutenant,' Byrnes said consolingly, 'as I don't intend to do what my father wishes.'

Looking at him for a long time, Slater said, 'It grieves me every bit as much as it does you, boy, but you don't have a choice.'

2

Ill from exhaustion, his body craving the alcohol it was so accustomed to, Roscoe Byrnes resigned himself to his fate. The hardship of travelling over rough terrain and sleeping under the stars had taken its toll on a man used to the soft life. Brought close to being a physical wreck, his homesickness for the security and familiarity of New York was approaching what he feared might be a mental breakdown. He had been watched over every minute of each day and night by Lt Slater and his two military underlings. Their hardships had increased on reaching and passing through an untamed Texas. For all his thinness and sick look, Lt Slater had remained totally unaffected by the heat, cold, dust, exertion, and danger from roaming bands of both white and red men.

They were in New Mexico now, entering the chaotic town of Mesilla. Confederate soldiers rubbed elbows with a bewildered civilian population. Cows foraged peacefully amidst the smoke of gun carriages burning from a recent battle. Women carried out every-day chores while infantry outfits drilled on sandy, makeshift parade grounds. Stores were being stacked, and three soldiers were cutting down the flagpole. After the long, wearying journey from New York, this scene of military activity completely dispirited Roscoe Byrnes.

As they rode into town, Slater had paused to ask a captain for directions. Now he reined up in front of a building that had the look of a schoolroom. One high corner of its stone walls had been blasted away by a shell. A picket stood at each side of the door, both with rifles and fixed bayonets. Dismounting, leaving Byrnes in the charge of his two subordinates, Slater passed unchallenged between the guards and went in through the doors.

As Byrnes and the others waited, a young soldier wandered up, studying them carefully. With a Texas drawl he asked, 'Are you men civilians, or what?'

'We're soldiers,' one of Byrnes's guards replied curtly.

'May God help you,' the Texan said sympathetically. 'I've wanted to be a soldier since I was knee-high to a milk-stool. Now I'm just about ready to hang up my fiddle, I've sure had enough of soldiering. They done promised us a uniform with a blue jacket, scarlet pants and a scarlet cap. That was going to be the jauntiest bit of headgear ever worn by a soldier-boy.' He broke off to indicate in disgust his uniform of grey cloth. 'Look what we got.'

It astonished Byrnes that the young soldier, who looked battle-weary, was not complaining about killing and bloodshed, but disappointment in the uniform he had been issued. His main grievance was not having been

25

given a silly cap. Such reasoning was incomprehensible to Byrnes.

He was trying to understand it when Slater came back out of the building. Transformed by the uniform he was now wearing, the lieutenant seemed to have gained physically and mentally. Smart and with a soldierly bearing, he came towards them, causing the Texas boy to throw up a hasty salute before running off.

'You've arrived at an historic time,' Lt Slater told Byrnes gravely. 'Yesterday, in command of just six hundred Texans, Lieutenant Colonel Baylor took this town and captured Major Isaac Lynde's entire command of Union troops. That was indeed a triumph for the Confederacy, and there will be many more. Major Byrnes is waiting inside for you, son. Go in, and take a real pride in becoming an officer in the Confederate States Army. You couldn't have chosen a better time, Byrnes.'

Not having chosen this or any other

time, a disgruntled Roscoe Byrnes dismounted and walked slowly to the building. His legs felt weak and shaky after being so long on horseback. The pride Slater had spoken of eluded him, and he felt only apprehension.

Inside the building, a sergeant stood bending over a table, sorting through papers. As dark-skinned as an Indian and obviously an outdoor man, the sergeant didn't look right in an office. After a cursory glance at Byrnes he totally ignored him. Byrnes walked towards the only other person in the room, a tall, stern-faced major.

Something strange was taking place inside of Roscoe Byrnes's head. Fragments of distant memories were colliding with each other before fitting together. A mind picture was forming which he was able to superimpose on the man he faced so as to recognize him, in a detached kind of way, as his father. Roscoe Byrnes searched his soul for some kind of warmth, some link of blood relationship. He found nothing.

For a moment it seemed that Major Byrnes was about to proffer a hand in greeting. But, every bit as ill-at-ease as his son, he cancelled the notion.

'There are many things a man would like to be different,' the major began in a pleasantly resonant voice, 'and this meeting between us is one I would wish to be different, very different.'

'It is not of my seeking, and I protest most strongly at my being treated in this way,' Roscoe Byrnes complained accusingly.

Reaching behind him, the major took a hand-written letter from a table. Making no attempt to read it, he held the letter up to support what he was about to say. 'Understandably, you blame me, Son, but I acted upon the request of your grandfather.'

Shaken by this, Roscoe found it difficult to credit that the genial old man in New York, the grandfather he was so close to, who got enjoyment from indulging him, could have brought about what he viewed as a disaster.

'I would never have believed this of my grandfather.'

'I assure you that it is true, Roscoe.' Major Byrnes spoke his name awkwardly, as if it was an alien word he had difficulty in pronouncing. 'My father, and I quote his words from this letter which I have learned by heart, feared that you were 'on the slippery slope to self-destruction'. He asked me to take you away from New York, Son, to make a man of you.'

Roscoe was taken aback. The resentment he had felt towards a father who had virtually abandoned him, and the sense of rebellion that had fostered in him since leaving New York suddenly lost impetus and direction, withering in him.

'Did he really see me in that light, sir?'

'I'm afraid that he did, Son,' Rutherford Byrnes answered sympathetically. 'Let me first say that I am mindful of my failings regarding you. I have always, especially on sleepless nights with a day on a battlefield behind me and another due to start at dawn, regretted not knowing my own son. So, as you can imagine, it caused me much heartache to read your grandfather's description of you.'

Though cutting him to the quick, this criticism stirred some of the old defiance in Roscoe. He said, 'I was living my life the way I wanted.'

'No, Son,' the major shook his head. 'You were living your life wrongly, but in the only way you knew how. Owney Byrnes's wealth was your undoing, Roscoe.'

'So you intend to run my life?'

'It is your life, Son, but, acknowledging that I have left it late, I do intend to help you,' Major Byrnes said, going on to explain. 'I am leaving Mesilla tonight, after seeing you sworn in as an officer in the Confederate Army. You will be given a uniform, Roscoe, something that you will learn to take pride in, and which in turn will teach you to value yourself.'

'What is there to prevent me, after you have left, from taking off the uniform and making my way back to New York?' a truculent Roscoe enquired.

'That wouldn't be wise,' the major answered. 'Firstly, we are at war. You would be classed as a deserter, hunted down and put to death by musketry. In the unlikely event of you avoiding that fate and surviving all the other innumerable hazards, you would reach New York to find that your grandfather would not advance you a single cent.'

'Then I have no option but to accept the rank and the uniform, sir,' Roscoe said reluctantly, 'but I warn you that I will never become a soldier.'

Looking him straight in the eye, his father said, 'I think otherwise. First impression aside, I see something in you that possibly even you don't realize is there. You will be placed in the capable hands of Sergeant Eli Whitman.' He nodded to where the sergeant had finished sorting papers and was half-sitting on a table. 'He's a good man, Son, an excellent soldier who is a veteran of the Mexican War. Allow him to be your tutor, your guide, your mentor, your friend and, above all, your conscience.'

'I will give the sergeant respect, sir, and I will take your oath, but, may God forgive me, I will not give the allegiance that I swear,' Roscoe warned, deciding it best to go along with his father's plan until the opportunity to desert presented itself. He was prepared to face any danger rather than become a soldier.

Expecting his father to be angered by what he had said, Roscoe was amazed to see him smiling. 'I think otherwise, Roscoe. Tomorrow, General Sibley will arrive here with an army of two-thousand three hundred men. He is marching northward, and you will be going with him. Now, have we left it too late for a father and son to shake hands?'

Taking the hand of his father,

who was in effect a stranger, was one of the oddest experiences of Roscoe's life. It was still painfully vivid in his mind the following morning when, stiff and uncomfortable in the uniform of a lieutenant, he stood at Sergeant Whitman's side watching a long, twisting, grey snake of marching soldiers approach. Comprised mainly of infantrymen, the column also contained artillery units pulling both light and heavy pieces.

'Are you angry at playing nursemaid to a reluctant soldier, Sergeant?' Byrnes asked Whitman as they squinted into the sun.

'No, sir,' the sergeant answered in crisp, military fashion. 'This duty got me out of that office, sir.'

'That may not be compensation enough when you discover that I have absolutely no interest in this army, or the war, Sergeant,'

Whitman chose his words carefully. 'When the war began, sir, the best families in the South rushed to secure commissions for their menfolk. I have had the misfortune to serve under a number of extremely inadequate officers, sir.'

'I should warn you,' Byrnes said with a laugh, 'that most of my life has been spent in the low dives of the Bowery and Broadway of New York, Sergeant.'

'Nevertheless, sir, my belief is that you will prove to be a chip off the old block, so to speak, sir. I was with Major Byrnes when we took this town, sir, and I have never seen a finer soldier in action. But might I suggest, sir, that you now go forward to meet General Sibley?'

Standing in a line of new officers waiting to be presented to Sibley, Byrnes, who knew no military discipline, studied the bearded general. He didn't like what he saw. General Sibley was plainly a man who had forsaken everything in life to dedicate himself to war. He had a harsh manner of speaking, and his grey eyes were cold, empty of all human feeling as he glared at Byrnes when he stepped casually in front of him.

'You have an insolent way with you, Lieutenant,' the general complained. 'Who are you?'

'I'm Roscoe Byrnes.'

'*Sir*, say *sir*!' An irate captain stepped forward, bringing his face close to that of Byrnes.

'Roscoe Byrnes, sir,' Byrnes said, mumbling the last word.

Glaring at him for some time, General Sibley said, 'You are not what I expect an officer to be, Byrnes. Make an old soldier happy by declaring that you have no connection with my old friend Rutherford Byrnes.'

'Major Byrnes is my father.'

'Man alive!' croaked General Sibley, too shaken to notice that Roscoe Byrnes had deliberately neglected to say 'sir'. He pointed a finger at Byrnes, 'I don't envy you, boy. I was at Charleston with your father when this fight began. You are a poor specimen to be fighting under the same flag. Living up to

Rutherford Byrnes's reputation will sure take some doing.'

'I don't intend to live up to anything but being Roscoe Byrnes.'

An angry lift of his head had Sibley's beard jut out pugnaciously, and his face became deep red before changing to purple. Rage made his words jerky and stilted. 'You are not only a fool, young Byrnes, but an arrogant fool, which is the worst kind of all.' He broke off to call his adjutant. 'Captain Leavis.'

'Sir.'

'I want this officer to go through an afternoon of intense training,' the general ordered, before addressing Byrnes once more. 'You will work long and hard for the remainder of this day, Lieutenant. In the morning we will march out from here, and you will be going with us. Report to me at first light and, I advise you to pay heed to what I am about to say, if you don't at that time conduct yourself in the manner of an officer, you will regret it.'

36

Dismissed by the irate general, Roscoe Byrnes had learned a valuable lesson: you can't buck the army. An hour later, as Captain Leavis commanded a training squad that included an out-of-condition, profusely sweating Byrnes, Eli Whitman confirmed for Byrnes that he had been foolish.

'It's best to appear to be going along with them, sir, even if you're not,' the sergeant advised, as they laboured stacking 128-pound shells for the Columbiads, 12-inch cannon that were to be used for practice firing.

The stiff breeze that blew into the muzzles of the guns and the faces of the soldiers, did nothing to cool Byrnes. In Byrnes's crew, working in a pretend-indolent manner that concealed the hard work he put in, was the boy Texan who had spoken to Byrnes the previous day.

'I didn't know you was an officer, sir,' the boy, whose name Byrnes learned was William Phillips, apologized for making that approach.

'Neither did I,' was Byrnes's laconic answer.

'You ain't like the rest of them, sir,' Phillips chuckled, amusement lighting up his freckled, boyish face.

'If you ever notice me getting like the rest of them, William, then you have my permission to shoot me,' Byrnes said.

'I couldn't do a thing like that, sir.'

'That's an order, William.' Byrnes was enjoying a natural rapport with the lad.

'Then I'll do it, sir,' an obedient but obviously lying Phillips came briefly to attention. Then he looked to where a browbeaten Negro boy slave was heading their way. 'Here comes Johnny S, sir. I hear he's going to be your servant.'

The gun was ready to fire, and a shout from Sergeant Whitman halted the black boy's approach. 'Stay there, boy.' As the slave stood beside a pile of cartridges, the sergeant asked Byrnes, 'Ready to fire, sir?'

About to reply that he didn't give a damn one way or the other, Roscoe Byrnes, aware that he was being closely scrutinized by Captain Leavis, rapped out an order. 'Fire!'

Whitman pulled the lanyard and the gun roared, belching flame and smoke. Something went wrong immediately. Too inexperienced to recognize the seriousness of what was happening, Byrnes saw the wind blow a smouldering piece of cartridge back toward the gun. Passing Whitman, Phillips and himself, the red-hot fragment landed on the pile of cartridges close to the Negro boy.

'Get down!' Sergeant Whitman shouted.

Transfixed, Byrnes heard William Phillips scream out a warning. 'Johnny S!'

Bemused, the young slave stood wide-eyed and unmoving. Phillips started to run toward the boy. Realizing that he couldn't reach him in time, the boy from Texas altered course. Veering to his left, he picked up a stick as he ran toward where the piece of shell glowed redly.

Watching Phillips poke the stick towards the fragment, intending to flick it off the shells, Byrnes was suddenly blown over by an explosion. Flat on his back on the ground, ears shrilly ringing, Byrnes was struggling to his feet when he realized that his new uniform was splattered with blood and slime. A high-pitched noise rose above the ringing in his ears, defeating it. Gagging on the acrid smell on the air, he saw that the noise was an endless, rising and falling scream coming from Johnny S. The boy was running round in a circle, his head back, white teeth gleaming as he cried out. Clasping his midriff, the slave was trying to hold in his entrails, but they were spilling messily over his hands.

A horrified Byrnes was relieved when the screaming suddenly switched off and the boy's run came to an end as he pitched forwards onto his face. Looking around for William Phillips,

Byrnes saw bits of the Texan scattered everywhere. When it came to him that the heavy wetness, the stickiness on his uniform had come from the shattered body of Phillips, Roscoe Byrnes started to run.

Aware of Eli Whitman trying to head him off, Byrnes evaded the sergeant and kept running. Blindly racing along an animal track through gorse bushes, he stopped to hold tightly with both hands to a waist-high rock as he vomited gushingly. When it was over, leaving him weak and with shaking legs, he staggeringly loped off.

Legs dragging, Byrnes weaved through a grove of trees that lined a creek. Dropping to his knees, he was too tired to reach for water to wash his face and hands with. Tearing at the soggy uniform, he sent buttons flying like bullets as he frantically ripped it from his body. Then he fell onto his side and curled up protectively, the noise of the explosion and the gruesome sights going on again and again in his head.

41

Sergeant Whitman found him there. He put a hand on Byrnes's shaking shoulder as he hunkered beside him. 'We'd better be going back to camp, sir.'

The black lad?' Byrnes enquired anxiously.

'Dead, sir; died soon after they got him to the hospital tent.'

Byrnes groaned. 'Those two boys, torn apart.'

'Like I said, sir, we'd better be heading back.'

'I can't go back, Sergeant.' Byrnes sat up, fighting an urge to be sick again.

Whitman said quietly, 'If you don't, sir, they'll send out a party to get you and you'll be shot at dawn. In the confusion of the explosion, Captain Leavis didn't see you go, sir. I can get you into camp, sir, fix you up with another uniform, and no one will know.'

'I know, Sergeant, and you know,' Byrnes said dully. 'Even if I wanted to — which I don't — I would never make a soldier. I can't put on another uniform after running like a coward.'

'What you did was neither new nor unique, sir,' the sergeant said.

'You mean it is a common reaction when someone sees something like that for the first time?' An ashamed Byrnes sought a reassuring answer.

'I still relive my first time in occasional dreams,' Eli Whitman confessed. 'It happened near the San Antonio river, at the old Spanish mission of Espada. I'd taken a blue-coat, one of General Cos's Mexican soldiers, prisoner. I was searching this Mex when he tried to jump me. I knifed him in self-defence, but he clung on to me and we fell over, him landing on top of me. As we fell, without me intending it, my knife sliced him wide open from top to bottom. That sure was a powerful mess, sir.'

'But you didn't run?'

Whitman shook his head. 'I was so sick that I blacked out. When

I came round I ran, sure enough. I must have bathed ninety times in the San Antonio, sir, but I couldn't get rid of the smell. I still don't feel clean today, sir.'

'Sergeant, let's get back to camp,' Byrnes said, getting shakily to his feet. 'That doesn't mean I'm going to accept the army, but I don't much like seeing myself as a coward.'

Stepping back to salute, Eli Whitman said, 'I just knew you are made of the same stuff as your daddy, Roscoe Byrnes.'

'Sir to you, Sergeant,' Byrnes reprimanded him jokingly.

'Yes, sir,' Whitman grinned, as he gave another salute.

3

'These are not even green soldiers, sir,' Sergeant Whitman complained worriedly, 'they are farm boys, totally unfit for combat.'

Although his military knowledge was strictly limited, Byrnes silently agreed. After he had passed muster with General Sibley, Byrnes had been assigned ten soldiers by the vindictive Captain Leavis before joining the general's march towards Valverde. They were heading for an engagement with Union General E.R.S. Canby to extend the Confederate Army's Far West campaign. But they had been halted by cannon fire from a concealed Union outpost up ahead. They were firing canisters filled with iron balls, creating a huge shotgun effect that was devastating to the advance units of Confederate troops. Byrnes had been ordered to form a skirmishing party to take out the Union cannon.

'They are no more inexperienced than I am, Sergeant,' Byrnes reasoned.

'Maybe so, but you aren't some damned fool of a boy, sir.'

No, I'm just a damned fool of a man who needs a drink, Byrnes thought ruefully. But he did share his sergeant's misgivings. Since he had arrived at Melissa there had been two deaths due to young soldiers playing foolish games with loaded muskets. Another had been stabbed through the heart with a bayonet during some tomfoolery. Leavis had deliberately selected the worst of a bad bunch for him.

'We'll have to make the best of what we've got, Sergeant,' a tense Byrnes said. His troops were huddled over, their clothing inadequate for this bleak February day. They were 'butternuts', so called because the standard grey uniforms were in short supply and they wore homespun dyed with butternut extract.

'We'll get by, sir,' Whitman predicted.

'I hope so,' Byrnes said. 'You're the soldier, Eli, so I'll follow you.'

'No, sir,' the sergeant said tersely. 'These boys have to see that you are in command. If they can't respect their officer, then they'll fall apart, sir.'

'I'll do my best,' Byrnes promised, overawed by the immense responsibility thrust upon him. 'Get the men ready to move out, Sergeant.'

'Sir,' Whitman accepted the order, pulling a gangling youth out of the line. 'You take the point, Bristow. You bring up the rear, Higgins.'

With the loose-kneed Bristow ahead of him, rifle held awkwardly rather than expertly, Byrnes went forward with his small unit. They moved along beside a head-height ridge. The sound of the cannon grew louder as they advanced. Starting up a slope that meant them having to crouch to remain concealed, they lost the protection afforded by the ridge. Byrnes halted his single-file column.

He eased himself up to cautiously peer over the ridge. Not far ahead he could see the flashes and smoke of the cannon. The terrain was rough and rocky enough to provide cover for an approach right up to the guns. The problem came from a flat, open stretch of some fifty yards between them and the start of the rocks.

'Not an easy one, sir,' Whitman commented.

'How do you see it, Sergeant?' Byrnes asked, completely at a loss as to how to proceed.

'If we come under fire out there, sir,' the sergeant answered, 'it will be from behind that square boulder. Somebody has to go across to take a look.'

'I'll go, Sergeant,' Byrnes said.

He had no stomach for it. In fact, he was filled with dread at the thought of showing himself to any Union troops. In a burst of fearful imagination he felt hot bullets tearing his body apart. But he lacked what it took to send someone else to what would probably be their death.

'You can't go, sir,' Whitman said. 'Call up Bristow and I'll tell him how to cross that ground.'

When Byrnes beckoned Bristow to them, the loose-jointed body of the callow youth was visibly shaking. Sergeant Whitman explained what was required of him.

'Cross that open ground at a run, Bristow, keeping low. Head for that cluster of rocks.'

'Are there any Federals out there?' Bristow enquired quakingly.

'That's what you're going to find out,' Eli Whitman said callously. 'You'll be able to see behind that square boulder. If there are no Yanks there, signal so by raising your right arm just once.'

Bristow went up over the ridge. He crossed the open ground in a bent-over run that would have been comical in different circumstances. Byrnes expected a crackle of gunfire to bring the boy down. But Bristow reached the rocks safely and threw himself behind them.

He and Whitman waited anxiously for a signal from Bristow. At last it came. A cinnamon-hued sleeved arm rose up from behind the rocks, just once.

'Right, you men,' Byrnes heard himself taking command. 'Move up here.'

'Is it safe?' a chubby, ruddy-faced boy called Warmor asked as he looked out over the open ground.

'The world stopped being safe for you when you left the farm, Soldier,' Whitman grunted. 'You men will go at intervals. Keep moving forwards and wait for me to slap your shoulder. Once you feel my hand, then get across there slicker than a snake and faster than a greased thunderbolt.'

The first soldier shot off at a crouching run, the single-strap haversack on his shoulder swinging from side to side. Watching him go, Byrnes, unnerved by the incessant roar of the cannon, quietly confessed to Whitman, 'I don't know how I'm going to be under fire, Sergeant.'

'Every man wonders about that his first time, sir,' the sergeant assured him. 'I'll be surprised if you let yourself down, sir.'

'I'll be surprised if I don't,' Byrnes said shakily and truthfully.

Whitman was ready to slap Warmor's shoulder. Now, just Higgins was left. Warmor went, and the powerfully-built Higgins moved up into position.

Hand raised above Higgins's thick shoulder, Whitman watched Warmor covering the final few yards, waiting for him to get behind the rocks. There was a sudden burst of rifle fire. Warmor stopped, coming out of his crouch to stand upright, acting as if he was marking time on the spot. Then his knees sagged and he crumpled to the ground.

'It's now or never,' Sergeant Whitman warned Byrnes and Higgins. 'Let's go!'

Byrnes, Whitman and Higgins ran,

going fast, zig-zagging this way and that as bullets kicked up the dust around their feet. Reaching Warmor, whose fleshy body was leaking blood into the sand, Byrnes slowed, but his sergeant yelled at him.

'He's dead, sir! Keep going!'

Incredibly, under such heavy fire, all three of them reached the cluster of rocks unharmed. The other soldiers were huddled together there, waiting for them. Byrnes dropped to his knees beside the troops, and Higgins was following suit when a bullet ricocheted off a rock close to Sergeant Whitman. Either the flattened bullet or a sliver of rock slashed across the sergeant's left thigh, slicing through the trousers and flesh. Whitman's feet went out from under him and he crashed to the ground.

'I can help him, sir,' Higgins said, as an uncertain Byrnes knelt by the sergeant, who was losing blood fast.

'I didn't think any of you boys had battle experience,' Byrnes said.

'We haven't, sir,' Higgins replied, 'but I've treated hurt animals and the like back home.'

'There weren't no Federals behind that boulder when I got here, sir,' Bristow called an apology.

'There sure is now,' another soldier said bitterly. 'Ask Harry Warmor.'

'Remain quiet you men,' Byrnes ordered as he watched Higgins's big hands work gently but firmly on Whitman's leg.

The Union troops had ceased firing their rifles, though the blasting of cannon continued. Moving Whitman to a half-sitting position, slicing the trouser leg open, Higgins fashioned a tourniquet out of a lanyard and put it around the sergeant's thigh above a long, open wound that pumped blood. Reaching up to take the pistol Whitman kept rammed in his belt, Higgins pushed the barrel into the lanyard and turned the gun to tighten it.

'Move my leg this way a bit, Higgins,' the tough sergeant ordered, 'so's I can reach to take the pressure off regularly.'

'Iffen you don't, that leg'll die, Sergeant,' Higgins warned.

'I know that, Soldier,' Whitman said, before turning his head to Byrnes. 'You can collect me here on the way back, sir. Those cannon have to be spiked, or a lot more of our boys are going to die back there.'

Watching the sergeant struggle to take his haversack off his shoulder, Byrnes fretted. With no idea of what to do, he admitted to his sergeant that neither did he know how to spike a gun.

'It's a simple job, sir,' Whitman said, as he pushed his bulging haversack towards Byrnes. 'There's plenty of soft wrought-iron nails in there. Use them.'

'How?' a bewildered Byrnes asked.

'I can show you, sir,' Higgins offered, as he put the finishing touches to treating the sergeant's wound.

'Is there anything that you don't know, Higgins?'

'There sure is one thing, sir.'

'What's that, Higgins?'

'How the blazes I came to be in this army in the first place,' Higgins replied wryly.

Surprising himself by being able to laugh, Roscoe Byrnes tried to form a plan of attack in a mind trained only how to secure the next drink or next woman. He found his thoughts wandering into worry over Cait Mackeever and pal Kit Geogheghan. His rapid transition from waster to warrior had been a shock to Byrnes's system. With an effort he brought his mind back to the present situation. That he would have to postpone any plan to escape from the army was a certainty. He could not desert either Whitman or these frightened boys.

Byrnes took a look around. The Union soldiers behind the large boulder had the advantage. There was no way to move up on either of their flanks without being seen.

Going over to Higgins, he asked, 'If you and me went straight at that boulder, do you think you're strong enough to help me up to the top?'

'I could throw you over the top if that was what you wanted, sir.' Higgins wasn't boasting but stating a fact.

'You're supposed to be on my side,' Byrnes grinned, liking this capable boy. If the two of them went straight towards the boulder the Union soldiers would have to come out round the sides to fire on them. It meant relying on the others to cover them. Byrnes pointed this out to Higgins, enquiring, 'How dependable is Bristow?'

'About the same as a fart in a whirlwind, sir,' was Higgins's scathing reply.

Discouraging though this was, Byrnes explained to Bristow that he and the other soldiers had to keep their rifles trained on the boulder, firing the instant a Union soldier appeared at either side.

'Have you got that, Bristow?' Byrnes asked.

'Yes, sir.' Bristow's big Adam's apple bobbed as he gulped.

Byrnes's doubts regarding the young soldiers were relieved by the injured but reliable Sergeant Whitman. Propped up a yard or two behind where Bristow and the others crouched, Whitman held a rifle aimed at Bristow.

'I can see that boulder from here, Bristow,' Sergeant Whitman warned. 'If just one Yankee pokes his hooter out and you boys don't fire at once, then, God help me, I'll shoot you in the back.'

'You got that, Bristow?' Byrnes questioned the frightened soldier.

'Yes, sir.'

Moving out, Byrnes and Higgins made good progress. For all his heavy build, Higgins was light on his feet. Reaching the boulder, which had a fairly smooth face and was some ten feet high, they propped their rifles against it, and the latter bent slightly to link the fingers of both hands to form a stirrup. Putting his left foot into Higgins's cupped hands, Byrnes was lifted up with ease and stretched his arms upwards to grasp the rim of the boulder. About to pull himself up, he heard Higgins's soft curse.

'Son of a bitch!'

Glancing down, Byrnes froze as he found himself looking into the black muzzle of a rifle held by a Union soldier who was cautiously easing out round a corner of the boulder. Unable to reach their rifles, Higgins and Byrnes were sitting ducks.

Being just seconds away from death didn't affect Byrnes in the way he would have expected. Looking at the strained expression on the face of the Northerner, who was no older than Higgins, he felt not fear but a strange feeling of relief. It shocked him to realize he seemed tired of life. Somehow it didn't matter that Bristow had let them down.

The sound of a shot from the

direction of the Confederates did nothing but make the Union soldier hesitate for a moment. He still held the rifle on them. Byrnes assumed that what he had heard was Whitman shooting Bristow as he had promised.

'Sir!'

Higgins's whispered exclamation came to Byrnes. He saw the Union infantryman do a part turn so that his back rested against the boulder. Then the young Yankee's body was giving way and he was sliding down, leaving a dark red smear of blood down the stone. The long rifle the soldier had been holding dropped to clatter down on the rocks.

Moving fast, Byrnes was up on top of the boulder and recovering his rifle. Placing it to one side, he lay flat on the boulder, reaching down to grasp the barrel of Higgins's rifle with both hands. Byrnes pulled hard as Higgins kept hold of his rifle and raised his legs to 'walk' up the boulder. It was tough going, for the boy was heavy, but Byrnes got him to the top.

Worn out, Byrnes fought an urge to lie on the boulder to rest. A life of wine, women and song wasn't the best conditioning for combat. Picking up their rifles, Higgins and he walked across the flat table-top of the rock. At the far edge they found themselves looking down on five terrified Union soldiers.

Caught without any option other than to fight, the Yankees were bringing up their rifles when Byrnes and Higgins opened fire. In a totally onesided fight, the five Union men were brought down swiftly and messily.

'I never killed a man before, sir,' Higgins said hollowly, as they made their way back across the boulder and prepared to climb back down.

'Neither have I, Higgins, neither have I,' Byrnes admitted, guessing that the boy felt as bad as he did. 'What's your first name, son?'

'Joe, sir.'

'Right, Joe,' Byrnes said warmly. 'I

see Bristow and the others are heading this way. We'd best go and get those cannon.'

As Byrnes quickly organized Bristow and the others into two columns with Higgins and himself taking the point, an icily biting wind was gaining strength. Making good time across the rough ground, Byrnes felt easier when they sighted the Union outpost. The cannon were behind low ramparts that had been constructed out of sand. Byrnes pointed to a solitary tree with its naked branches bending and twisting in the wind.

'Do you think you could take a look from up there, Joe?' he asked.

'Give me five minutes, sir,' the willing Higgins said.

Byrnes watched the boy climb the tree, clinging on as the strong wind whipped through the thin material of his makeshift uniform. Reaching a high-up fork, Higgins straddled it. Bracing his back against the main trunk of the tree, he studied the distant gun emplacement for a time. Then he swung down to the ground with the agility of a squirrel.

'There's just ten artillerymen, sir,' Higgins reported.

This pleased Byrnes. The only infantry protecting the cannoneers must have been those Higgins and he had dealt with back at the boulder. He enquired, 'Can we get above them or flank them, Joe?'

With a negative shake of his head, Higgins answered, 'There's no high ground, sir.'

'We can't wait until dark,' Byrnes said with regret. 'They'll have done too much damage back there by then.'

'I don't know how much of a fight they'll be able to put up, sir. That wind's whistling in across there and them Yankees look to be plumb frozen.'

'They could still pick us off while we're out in the open,' Byrnes said, before a thought made him ask Higgins, 'You know what happened back in Mesilla, Joe, when William Phillips and that black boy were killed?'

'I heard about it, sir,' a puzzled Higgins replied. Then he grasped what Byrnes was thinking. 'I understand, sir. While you and the others keep them busy, you want me to sneak in round the side and fire their powder.'

'Actually, I was going to put you in charge up front, Joe, while I went in from the side.'

'I hate to argue with an officer, sir,' Higgins began, 'but without you Bristow and the others are sure likely to run. That would leave you and me on our lonesome with them Federal artillerymen. Better I do the blasting.'

This made sense, and Byrnes accepted it with a nod. Speed was of the essence, and he explained to the others what was required of them. Then they spread out, using whatever cover they could in an advance on the artillery emplacement.

When they were in close enough, Byrnes ordered his men to commence rapid fire to cover Higgins as he crawled away at an angle. The roar of the cannon ceased at once, but the Confederate rifle fire was not returned.

But then the Federals did respond. As Byrnes saw Joe Higgins disappear, so did a withering fire commence to keep Byrnes and his men pinned down. Aware that they had lost the initiative, Byrnes, untrained but intelligent, knew that Higgins was doomed if some move wasn't made to occupy the attention of the Federal soldiers. The only scheme he could come up with bordered on the suicidal. He shouted to Bristow and the others:

'On my count of three, men, stand up and advance, firing from the hip as you go. That should keep their heads down.'

Reaching 'three' and getting to his own feet, Byrnes feared that his gamble had failed. As his nine men stood, four immediately fell dead. But with the other five soldiers and he firing from the hip as they walked forwards, it was the turn of the Union soldiers to take cover.

One Yankee knelt and raised his rifle to his shoulder. They were close enough for Byrnes to see the colour of the Northerner's eyes before one of their bullets flattened him face first across the rampart.

A second Union soldier died, dramatically and noisily. Then a musket was raised with a piece of white rag tied to the barrel.

'Cease firing, but keep them covered,' Byrnes ordered.

Eight Union troops rose up unsteadily, hands raised high, fear on their faces. Byrnes was about to call them forward when there was a terrific explosion behind them. Flame and smoke bellowed up, the ear-splitting roar so confusing that Byrnes's mind was only able to register what was happening in a series of jerky, disconnected scenes.

The eight surrendering Union soldiers had been blown high, the explosion ripping limbs from bodies. His own men were knocked off their feet, but were coming upright, blackened and bemused but uninjured. A jagged shell fragment slashed open his left hand from knuckle to wrist.

Fearing for Higgins, Byrnes went over the rampart, slipping and sliding on the mashed remains of men. He passed three cannon that had been capsized and damaged by the explosion.

Racing to a gaping hole in the ground that had to have been the site of the ammunition store, he looked frantically around for Higgins. All he could see was burnt grass and scorched earth. Widening his search, he came to a charred body which the blast had stripped naked. Steeling himself, he bent to grasp a shoulder on which the skin had been burnt as crisp as bacon. Gently pulling the corpse onto its back, Byrnes discovered that the wrecked face didn't even resemble that of a human being, but the shape of the head convinced him that it was Joe Higgins. The able young Confederate had died in an explosion of his own making.

Releasing the shoulder, Byrnes stood upright. Feeling desolate, he saw blood dripping steadily from his cut hand. These bleak and hostile surroundings were a far cry for the New York barrooms he was accustomed to. Then he jumped like a startled rabbit as he felt fingers on his shoulder. They were fingers that tugged at the strap of Eli Whitman's haversack filled with nails.

'I'd better carry that, sir. You look right done in.'

Pivoting on his heel, Byrnes found himself facing a smiling Joe Higgins. The boy's makeshift uniform had been singed and there were dark patches on his face where gunpowder had been burnt in, but he seemed otherwise unharmed.

Gesturing toward the wrecked cannon, Higgins said regretfully, 'I guess I'm not going to be able to show you how to spike a gun after all, sir.'

4

Ordered by Captain Leavis to escort Eli Whitman to the surgeon's wagons in the rear echelon, where he would get his own hand treated, Byrnes was mentally confused. Once he had safely delivered Whitman he would have a perfect chance of escaping from the army. But now a feeling of pride in his recent military achievement was equalling his desire to flee. Eli Whitman had been the first to praise him.

'I knew right off that you were a chip off the old block, sir,' the sergeant had enthused. 'You were born to soldier, sir, just like your daddy.'

Byrnes doubted that Whitman was right. If he had been born to soldier, then why had it been necessary for him to be forced into the army? Yet the admiration of his sergeant combined with other things to make Byrnes feel good. The sense of purpose in leading the assault had dynamically concentrated his hitherto fragmented personality. Not only did he like himself for the first time ever, but he now despised the Roscoe Byrnes of the New York era. The resulting mental turmoil was perplexing. He found there was a confidence-shaking insecurity about having no plan for the immediate future.

With the injured Whitman painfully jostled by the 'avalanche', the two-wheeled, springless ambulance on which he rode, they paused on the crest of a hog's back. A dismayed Byrnes couldn't take in everything that was happening on the treeless stretch of ground below them. The medical wagons had been lined up in haste and haphazardly. Bloodied surgeons toiled, working at top speed. The injured who lay waiting in long lines, were far outnumbered by the rows of dead. A patch of ground to the right was covered with dead horses.

Byrnes estimated there had to be at least forty.

He was staggered. Just three cannon had caused all this suffering and death. What would it be like when the Confederates now advancing on the Union positions engaged the enemy?

As they arrived, an elderly surgeon with tired eyes left off tending what looked like a corpse. Body sagging with weariness, he walked over to take a look at Whitman's leg.

'You'll live, Sergeant,' the surgeon said dully.

'Any chance of you fixing me up pronto, Doc?' Eli Whitman asked. 'We're just about to hit them Yankees up yonder, and I want to be in that fight.'

Shaking his head in despair, the surgeon pointed absently to where a mound of dead bodies had been stacked. He complained, 'Why don't you just crawl over and join them, Sergeant? It would save me and a lot of others a whole heap of trouble, for that's where you'll finish up anyway.'

'I'm not here for a lecture, Doc, but to get my leg fixed,' Whitman muttered.

'I know what you're here for, Sergeant,' the surgeon said, reaching for Byrnes's injured hand and looking at it. 'That won't take a lot of fixing, Lieutenant,' he said, turning his head to shout over his shoulder. 'Cora!'

Until that moment Byrnes hadn't noticed there were three female nurses present. They knelt, helping to ease the pain of the wounded and bring comfort to the dying. At the doctor's call, one of them, petite, dark-haired and pretty, stood and walked over to join them.

'Take care of the lieutenant's hand for me please, Cora,' the surgeon said.

Coming close, head bowed, face averted, the girl held Byrnes's hand for a moment, studying it. Then she said, 'Please, come with me.'

'What about me, Doc?' Whitman pleaded, as Byrnes followed the nurse.

'Don't worry, Sergeant,' the surgeon

71

said wearily. 'I'll put your leg back on so's you can go get your damned-fool head blown off.'

As he walked behind the nurse towards a wagon, Byrnes caught the odour of the ether being used in the operations going on around him. Then he was breathing in something very different, a gut-wrenching stench that made him use his good hand to partially block off his nose and mouth. Even when filtered in this way the smell was unbearable.

Curious, he looked around, and his stomach churned as he identified the source of the foul odour. A hole had been dug a little way off, into which had been thrown the arms and legs of soldiers as they were lopped off by surgeons.

'My God, ma'am,' Byrnes gasped as they reached the back of a wagon and the nurse took a bottle of antiseptic and some bandages from a box, 'how long did it take you to be able to stand this?'

As she cleansed his wound, she answered softly, 'Until a few months ago, Lieutenant, I was a schoolteacher. I am far from accustomed to such terrible injuries.'

'Then why are you doing this work?' he asked, not prying but interested as he made a circular motion with his wrist to facilitate her bandaging.

'Why are you a soldier, Lieutenant?' she countered with a question of her own.'

'I didn't have any other choice.'

'Neither did I,' she replied seriously. 'I've always felt a need to help people less fortunate than myself.' She looked around her at the rows of injured, dying and dead men. 'Though I hate what is happening in this war, I want to do what I can for these poor souls.'

'It wasn't a matter of conscience in my case, ma'am,' Byrnes said in part explanation, adding nothing further.

Completing the neat bandaging of his arm, she looked up at him. 'My conscience doesn't motivate me,

Lieutenant. It may strike you as sanctimonious, but I am convinced that nursing is my calling.'

What she said and the way she said it reminded him of the crusading religious girls back home. They would endure the obscene sights and lurid language of New York's lowest dives, seemingly oblivious to everything other than a passion to entice poor sinners to repentance and salvation. Probably because he had been beyond help, a hopeless, helpless excuse for a man, the fervour of those brave girls had embarrassed him then, just as the courage of this nurse was doing now.

Uncomfortable, Byrnes looked to where a captain and a corporal, the former with his head wrapped in a bloody bandage, the latter with one arm in a sling, drilled a small squad of soldiers. The uniforms of the men were ripped, muddy and bloody. They obeyed the sergeant's commands so physically awkwardly that it was plain they had all been wounded in some way.

'When this war ends, ma'am, so will your calling,' Byrnes observed.

'No,' she emphatically replied. 'When that happens I shall seek out other wars, wherever they may be, and offer my services.'

'That's a real noble ambition, ma'am,' he said, impressed. 'I feel that you will make a name for yourself one day. What name should I be looking out for?'

'I'd like to accept that as a compliment, Lieutenant,' she answered demurely, 'but I fear that you are making fun of me.'

'I really meant what I said, ma'am.'

'Then my name is Cora Graycot,' she said with a faint blush, holding her right hand out formally to him. 'I have never met a soldier quite like you, Lieutenant.'

Taking her hand, he answered, 'That is because I am not a real soldier, Miss Graycot.'

'Maybe that is what you think, but I am sure that you will one day be famous,' she told him with an arch look before turning the tables on him. 'What name should I expect to see in the headlines, Lieutenant?'

'I am Roscoe Byrnes.'

'Lieutenant Roscoe Byrnes,' she said slowly and distinctly, like she was testing the sound of his name on her own lips.

The silence that followed this exchange was unsettling them both, then the corporal wearing a sling marched up smartly.

'Major Fitzpatrick's compliments, sir.' The corporal saluted. 'He would appreciate it if you could join him for a few moments, sir.'

Reluctantly releasing the hand of the nurse, Byrnes made a bow. 'I am most thankful to you for tending my wound, Miss Graycot. My hope is that we will meet again.'

'You are welcome, Lieutenant Byrnes, and I am certain that one day we shall see each other once more.' The wistful way she said these words betrayed her true thoughts. With the raging battles to come, the chances of them ever meeting again were remote.

This dismal thought was still with Byrnes when he saluted Major Fitzpatrick. The wound to the senior officer's temple seemed to have become infected, spreading downwards so that the left side of his face was grotesquely swollen and discoloured. When the major spoke, only the right side of his mouth opened, the left side of his face staying stiffly immobile.

Returning the salute, Fitzpatrick said, 'I understand that you will be rejoining General Sibley at once, Lieutenant . . . ?'

'Byrnes, sir,' Byrnes volunteered his name. 'Yes, sir.'

Looking at the chaos around him, Fitzpatrick sighed. 'It will be at least two days before we are ready to follow the main body, Byrnes. We will await the arrival of the rear echelon, so as to hand over the seriously wounded. As the general will require every available man for the coming fight, I request that you take this squad of walking wounded back with you.'

'Sir,' Byrnes had to agree.

Not relishing the thought of leading twelve disgruntled men back into a war that had already caused them to suffer, Byrnes had the squad stand easy while he sought out his sergeant. Eli Whitman lay on an improvised operating table that had been clumsily constructed out of a wagon tailgate, his leg being operated on by the exhausted surgeon of earlier.

When he told Whitman that he was leaving, he couldn't understand the reply because the sergeant was chewing hard on a piece of wood. Byrnes looked questioningly at the surgeon, who was using a large, obviously dirty needle to sew Whitman's thigh together.

'We're out of both ether and chloroform,' the doctor explained. 'All I have to offer is a bullet or a lump of timber to bite on.'

Wincing inwardly as he tried to imagine the agony Whitman must be experiencing with only a piece of wood for an anaesthetic, Byrnes laid a hand on the sergeant's shoulder, saying, 'Catch up with us soon, Eli.'

Walking away, a shout from Whitman had him turn. When he looked back the surgeon was still at work, but the sergeant had taken the wood out of his mouth, holding it in one hand as he called, 'I'll be back with you, sir, as soon as the doc's stitched the last stitch.'

Acknowledging this with a wave of his good hand, Byrnes moved on to collect his squad. They were a bunch of resentful young men who spoke not a word to him unless he addressed one individually. Even then he got the barest of answers, and they all grew more morose as first the roar of artillery came to them. As they plodded on, so did the unmistakable sounds of battle fill the air.

Their first contact with the Confederate States Army came with the sighting of artillery equipment. The battleground was such that there was no room at the rear of the guns, so the caissons and limbers had been left on a flat piece of heavily wooded ground.

With the bombardment of Valverde in full swing when he arrived, Byrnes found Lt Slater in charge of a battery of 10-inch Columbiads mounted as mortars. The noise near the guns was deafening, while up ahead shot and shell smashed into the enemy positions. A stormy dark sky was frequently spattered by the quick light from bursting shells.

'Just in time,' Slater shouted a greeting over the roar of the guns. 'We've been at it for hours, so the infantry will be moving off soon.'

Beckoning his reluctant squad forward in readiness, Byrnes, too inexperienced to know what military question to ask, shouted, 'What's the situation, Lieutenant Slater?'

'There's two thousand three hundred of us,' Slater, his voice hoarse from continuous shouting, called back, 'and the Union troops number three thousand eight hundred.'

'What does that mean?' the raw Roscoe Byrnes asked.

'That they out-number us by fifteen hundred men,' Slater grinned, enjoying giving the obvious answer. His face went serious as a runner came up to him and he bent to listen to what the sweating soldier had to report.

Then, shouting the cease-fire order, Slater paused, adjusting to a new and profound silence that was, in its own way, as disturbing as the gunfire it replaced. Then he addressed Byrnes. 'You'd better find Captain Leavis, Byrnes. Take these men of yours with you. It's time for the infantry to get going.'

'I wish I was back in New York,' Byrnes grumbled.

'I'm glad that you're not, Roscoe.'

Unable to believe that Slater had

spoken those words, a dismayed Byrnes looked back at the officer who up until now had held a base opinion of him.

'Good luck,' Slater said with a friendly smile.

Beckoning the party of walking wounded to follow him, Byrnes, more bewildered than ever by what was happening to him, sought Captain Leavis among the apparent chaos that precedes any military action.

Putting Byrnes in command of a unit, Leavis ordered, 'See that the men you brought back with you are issued rifles, Lieutenant. We move out in ten minutes. We're outnumbered, and General Canby is expecting us, but our artillery has hammered them. It is essential that we hit the enemy while he's still reeling.'

The fact that Leavis had treated him as an experienced soldier amazed Byrnes every bit as much as Slater's camaraderie had. In a short time the opinions of those about him had changed drastically. He wished that he could regard himself as positively as Captain Leavis and Lt Slater now did.

'Good to see you back, sir.'

Joe Higgins who was in his squad, grinned in pleasure as he greeted Byrnes. Bristow was there, too, skulking in the background, the memory of the perilous attack on the Union gun emplacement still too frightening for him to welcome the lieutenant who had brought him face to face with death.

'Help me get these boys fitted up with rifles, Joe,' Byrnes said.

When this had been done, Captain Leavis gave the 'fixed bayonets' order and they were on their way.

The attack was launched in three ranks, with Byrnes and his command in the centre of a line that stretched out over a long distance on either side of him. They went at walking pace so as not to tire the troops for the fighting which lay ahead. The 18-inch-long bayonets with triangular-shaped blades affixed to the rifles forecast that it would be hand-to-hand combat. Higgins, who paced at his side, remarked on this.

'I heard some of them men talking, sir, and I don't reckon fixing bayonets was a good idea. Them that know say that just the thought of using those things makes them feel queasy, sir.'

'I can understand that, Higgins,' Byrnes said, 'but don't let these boys hear you say it. We don't want them running off.'

'No, sir. Sorry, sir.'

They remained silent then, the rhythm that came with keeping in step making their walk seem effortless. The storm that had been threatening for some time, suddenly broke. A strong wind whipped stinging rain into their faces as they plodded on. Byrnes saw the pass up ahead where the Union Army would be lying in wait. It was made sinister by the shadow of a volcanic plug that must have reached up to around 1,500 feet above the desert. As the air was suddenly filled with a screeching of shells, the Confederates loudly cheered. They believed that their artillery had opened up again to support them before they came within range of the enemy.

Though no more battle experienced than they were, Byrnes doubted that they were right. His guess was that the shells were coming from the Union lines. He was proved right, in a truly horrible way, when a series of explosions behind them peppered their backs with clumps of earth and fragments of stone.

Looking over his shoulder, Byrnes saw that the shells had cut a swathe through the centre and rear ranks following. Wounded men were crying out for help, dying men were shrieking, and the already dead lay quietly where they had fallen.

'The Yankees are hitting us with twelve-pounder howitzers, sir,' Higgins shouted, yet again revealing a knowledge of things military that he shouldn't possess.

'Charge!' Captain Leavis shouted. 'Double-quick time!'

Rifles held at the ready, bayonets slicing through the wet air, the Confederates charged over the remaining distance between them and the enemy. The Union shelling continued, but Ross Byrnes instantly grasped Leavis's strategy. The explosions were happening too far behind to cause damage now. They were out-running the bombardment, and the Yankee cannoneers had no time to shorten their range.

Delighted by this, the running soldiers cheered. It was muddy underfoot now, and they slipped and slid as they went, but the lines didn't waver. But with rain beating hard against them, the men at each end of the first line found themselves floundering in soft, marshy ground. The firm ground continued to narrow. The advance was slowed as the Confederate soldiers were forced to bunch up, and panic set in, becoming worse as the Yankee cannoneers took advantage of the delay by resetting the range of their guns.

Grapeshot was once again causing casualties among the Confederate assault force. The advance had stalled. Byrnes joined the other officers in trying to restore order. But they failed until Captain Leavis pushed his way to the front.

Though he had no cause to like the captain, Byrnes was filled with admiration for him as he took over, instantly raising morale. A despondent boy soldier stood holding the Confederate flag loosely so that it dangled in the mud. Snatching it from him, Leavis waved the flag and a mighty cheer went up. Holding the flag high as he passed it back to the soldier, he sent the lad running forward, drawing his own sword in a symbolic gesture as he ran towards the Union defences.

Cheering again, seeming to naturally adjust to the narrowness of firm ground, the Confederates restarted their advance, following the courageous Leavis.

But the Federal defenders were ready for them. Captain Leavis was within 100 yards of the Union lines, with Byrnes and the others close behind him, when a devastating fusillade of rifle fire was added to the death and destruction caused by the cannon.

The boy with the flag fell, mortally wounded. Bending to take the flag from him, Leavis passed it to another soldier, gesturing for him to hold it high and proudly.

With brave men being brought down fast, the Confederate advance continued apace. Then grapeshot tore the body of the flag-carrying soldier to shreds. Retrieving the flag once more, Leavis this time didn't look for a replacement. With his sword in one hand and the flag waving in the other, he kept going a military advance that would have faltered and come to a stop without the inspiration he provided.

They were within yards of engaging the enemy in close-quarter combat when disaster struck. Byrnes, fired with an enthusiasm he wouldn't have suspected he possessed, was urging his men forward when he saw Captain Leavis's sword go flying up into the air. Next he saw the captain's knees buckling. Turning as he fell, Leavis put a smashed, bloody chest on display. There could be no doubt that he was dead, and the advance halted, despite Byrnes and his fellow officers yelling at the men.

Then the lean figure of Lt Slater came charging to the front. Under heavy fire, Slater reached where Leavis had fallen. Bending to grip the flag, he couldn't tug it from the grasp of the dead captain. Gripping the flag in both hands, placing a foot on Leavis's wrist, Slater at last gained the flag and held it aloft, giving a rebel yell as he did so.

The war cry of the Confederacy was swiftly taken up by the men, who charged after the flag-waving Lt Slater. With the firm ground widening to the left and the right, the Confederates spread out to attack all along the Union defensive line. Now an unstoppable force, demoralizing the enemy with the impetus of their onslaught and incessant, wild rebel yells, General Sibley's men quickly gained the advantage.

At the front throughout, firing his pistol, surprised to find how easily he took to battle, Roscoe Byrnes, with an able Joe Higgins at his side, played a vital part in the fight.

Suffering heavy losses, the Union soldiers stood it for a while. Then they began an orderly retreat that turned into a shambles as the Confederates pursued them. What had been a desperate all-day battle became a complete rout. As the Yankees withdrew Lt Slater called a halt.

'Victory is ours, boys,' Slater hollered, his normally dour face glowing.

General Sibley came riding up, his horse doing a finicky manoeuvring through the wounded and dead soldiers that were strewn around. Smiling, he informally saluted individuals and groups of men.

'We have been victorious, men,' he cried. 'We are on our pathway to the Pacific Ocean.'

'We've lost Captain Leavis, General,' Lt Slater reported, using a hand to indicate where the former adjutant's body lay twisted in the mud.

'Damned shame,' a genuinely upset General Sibley looked down at the body. 'Captain Leavis was an excellent officer, Lieutenant, and I will sorely miss him. But the war goes on, *Captain* Slater.'

'Captain, sir?' an uncertain Slater questioned.

'Promotion in the field, Captain Slater. You are my new adjutant,' Sibley announced before twisting a little in the saddle to look down on Byrnes. 'You didn't escape my notice, Lieutenant, and you proved to me that you have ability. You will assume the duties formally carried out by Captain Slater.'

'Sir.' Acknowledging this recognition. Byrnes was warmed by it. Previously believing that he would never forgive his father for abducting him from New York, he was now ready to thank him for making his life meaningful. Sure that he was being insubordinate, he asked, 'Might I make a request relating to promotion in the field, sir?'

Though either curiosity or annoyance caused him to frown, General Sibley gave what could be described as an affable nod of permission.

'It's about Higgins, sir,' Byrnes said, placing a hand on Higgins's wide shoulders. 'He's a good soldier, sir, with talents that are wasted as a private.'

Studying Byrnes intently, then Higgins, before bringing his steady gaze back to Byrnes. 'You learn quickly, Lieutenant Byrnes, which is to your credit, even though you transgress the rules of rank. Nevertheless, you would not be the son of Rutherford Byrnes if you didn't display individualism.

You are requesting that Higgins be promoted to the rank of sergeant?'

'I am suggesting that, sir, not requesting it,' Byrnes made a respectful qualification.

'I'll go part-way with you, Lieutenant. It is a foolish general who doesn't pay heed to his junior officers, but a weak general who grants their every request. I am neither of the two, so from this moment on that young fellow of yours will be Corporal Higgins.'

'Thank you, sir,' Byrnes said, rewarded by the happy smile that Joe Higgins was unable to conceal.

Preparing to leave, General Sibley spoke to Slater as he reined his horse to the left. 'The hospital wagons are on their way, Captain Slater. Once everything is attended to here, I want the men got ready for our next objective, which is Albuquerque.'

'Sir.' Slater accepted the order.

'There is no stopping us now, Captain,' Sibley said joyfully as he rode away. 'We are going to march all the way to the Pacific.'

Hearing this, Byrnes felt a rush of anticipation due to his new-found military interest. But this elation was surpassed by a sense of excited expectation of seeing Cora Graycot.

5

General Sibley's predictions had been
proved correct. The Confederate battle
triumphs had continued. First Albuquerque had fallen and then the
Southerners had marched on to occupy
Santa Fe without opposition. Here the
Southern army of occupation had set
up a tented camp and was ready to
go out on the town. First the soldiers
had to attend the official celebration,
where Byrnes was having his first taste
of alcohol since being forcibly removed
from New York. The dead of both sides
had been buried, the wounded tended
to, and the Union prisoners-of-war
rounded up and placed in a specially-
built compound on the outskirts of
town. Eli Whitman had rejoined the
unit in time to play a significant part
in the fight for Albuquerque. The
sergeant and Corporal Joe Higgins had

become Roscoe Byrnes's constant and loyal companions both on and off the battlefield. They accompanied him now as General Sibley entered to a mighty cheer from his troops.

The venue was a huge building, recently constructed for some military purpose by a Union Army that hadn't had time to use it. Built of pine logs buttressed with palmettos, the whole structure was strapped with iron. The front-facing wall was pierced with four 'windows' for cannon. The Union troops had left the massive building empty except for a solitary 8-inch columbiad. The gun now stood as a symbol of victory on a stage that had been hastily and crudely erected against the rear wall. General Sibley, a smartly turned out Captain Slater at his side, rested a hand on the cannon as he made a speech to his soldiers.

Not hearing much of what the general said, Byrnes was preoccupied with the changes in himself that he was noticing with increasing frequency. There was an abundance of liquor available here, but he had taken only a few sips from one glass. Back in New York, so short a time ago, he would have been roaring drunk by this time.

He caught the end of Sibley's speech ' . . . and have lost comrades, fellows-in-arms you had come to love. Proficient though we may be, and soldiers to the core, prolonged acquaintance with the battleground wearies us all. Great times, great conquests lie ahead for us, gentlemen, but right now Santa Fe is a blooming garden of social refreshment compared with the wilderness of combat. Military discipline has been relaxed so that you may feel free to enjoy yourselves this night, men.'

As the soldiers cheered and applauded wildly, Sergeant Whitman leaned close to Byrnes to ask confidentially, 'What about you, sir? You could leave here tonight and head right back to New York.'

'Don't think I haven't given that

some thought, Eli,' Byrnes replied. 'But I've got a hankering to see a bit more of this war.'

'Like I said before, sir, you were destined to be a soldier,' Whitman said with a pleased grin.

'You would seem to know me better than I know myself, Sergeant,' Byrnes commented wryly.

Up on the stage Sibley and Slater stepped to one side and a young soldier with a good voice led the community singing of 'Dixie's Land', the most popular song among Southern soldiers. Male voices rose in concert to fill the huge arena stirringly. It was in sharp contrast to the singing of bawdy songs in Byrnes's hedonistic days. Slipping into an introspective mood, he thought of Cait Mackeever. He hoped that the Bowery Bastille had survived the police crackdown. It would be reassuring to know that Cait would be there when he returned to New York, but it grieved him that Kit Geogheghan wouldn't be. Eli Whitman and Joe Higgins were comrades and brave men he could rely upon, but, though he was growing close to both those soldiers, they could never be substitutes for Kit. Over the years the two of them had shared so much that an almost magical bond existed between them. But Geogheghan had long been a target for Police Captain Silver, and now that the City Fathers had decided on a clean-up, Byrnes's friend would have been forced either into hiding or to leaving town.

The song had changed now to 'The Bonnie Blue Flag'. Joe Higgins was eagerly joining in, but Whitman was silent, smiling a knowing smile at Byrnes. Puzzled at first by the sergeant's obvious amusement, Byrnes understood as Cora Graycot came up to them. Dressed in a red merino shirt with a wide belt and black skirt, dark hair swept up from her forehead in the pompadour style, she was barely recognizable as the woman he had seen kneeling among injured soldiers. She had been lovely then, but now she was truly beautiful.

'When I forecast that we would meet again, Lieutenant Byrnes,' she smiled, 'I should have warned you that I am a witch.'

'That I could never believe, but you certainly are bewitching,' he said gallantly, taking her hand and holding it in both of his.

'I have been following close behind you, Lieutenant, and my prayers have been with you,' Cora told him, face serious, eyes holding his. 'What I have heard about your heroism and daring, Lieutenant Byrnes, I do believe that you told me a fib when you denied being a soldier.'

'It is the truth, Miss Graycot,' Byrnes insisted. 'You ask my sergeant . . . oh, forgive me, this is Sergeant Whitman, and the young warbler here is Corporal Joe Higgins. They are two friends I owe everything to, including my life.'

Acknowledging both soldiers with a friendly smile, she asked, 'Well, Sergeant Whitman, would you say that Lieutenant Byrnes isn't really a soldier?'

'That's a tricky question, ma'am,' Whitman frowned. 'What I would say is that he's the most soldierly non-soldier I've ever soldiered with, if that makes any sense at all.'

'It doesn't,' Cora laughed, 'but I believe I have caught the meaning behind it.'

'Are you with the wagons behind the tented camp, Miss Graycot?' Byrnes enquired.

'Technically, yes, but I'm not living there. General Sibley arranged accommodation for the other two nurses and myself at the Leland Hotel.'

Having seen the hotel as he'd come into town, Byrnes, who was finding it difficult to remember what sleeping in a proper bed was like, made a snap decision. Turning to Higgins, he said. 'Go along to the hotel, Joe, and book a room each for Eli Whitman, yourself and me.'

'I'll do as you say for you and Sergeant Whitman, sir, but not for myself,' Higgins replied. 'All I gets paid is eighteen dollars a month, and I ain't seen a cent of that yet.'

'You'll be my guest, Joe. Here, pay in advance.' Byrnes took money from his pocket and passed it to Higgins before bringing his attention back to Cora Graycot. 'It's a real long time since I dined with a lady, Miss Graycot. I'd be honoured if you'd join me at — '

'Sir! Sorry to break in, sir,' Whitman said urgently, 'but isn't there something real familiar about that major who's just joined the general?'

Looking to the stage where a major was sharing a pumping handshake with Sibley, Byrnes gave a gasp of surprise. 'My father!'

There was a question in the eyes Cora turned on him, but Byrnes had no time to deal with it because something else was happening. Captain Slater had been moved forward on stage, and General Sibley was addressing the assembly.

'In the past few weeks there have been many acts of bravery, actions above and beyond what any army can either expect or ask of a man. In due course those of you who have done the Confederate States Army proud will receive fitting awards for your courage. But, in the meantime, there are still fights to be fought, and I have a duty to provide you with the most able commanders for the tasks that lie ahead. With this in mind, I announce that Captain Slater will now assume the rank of major.'

Slater was a popular and respected officer who deserved the applause he received from the troops in the hall. But Sibley was holding up both hands to quell the clapping. When it had died down, he gestured toward Major Rutherford Byrnes.

'A lot of you have had the good fortune to serve under Major Byrnes. Those who have, and you others who have only heard his name spoken in awe wherever soldiers gather, will know that it is right and fitting for Major Byrnes to become Colonel Byrnes.'

This time the applause was polite rather than enthusiastic, and far from prolonged. General Sibley squinted down at the audience. 'I believe that Lieutenant Roscoe Byrnes is with us.'

'This sounds like good news,' Cora Graycot smiled at an uncomfortable Byrnes.

'Probably going to announce that he'll be shot at dawn,' Whitman predicted with a grin.

Byrnes had made no move, but Slater was pointing down at him, calling out an invitation that had more than the hint of an order to it. 'Come on up Liuetenant Byrnes.'

Up on the stage, a self-conscious Byrnes was met by his father, who asked, 'Will you permit me to shake you by the hand, Son?'

Never having been one to push himself forward unless drunk, Roscoe Byrnes, cold sober, was both embarrassed and disorientated by what was happening. Sibley waited just long enough for the father-and-son handshake to be completed, then placed a hand on the younger Byrnes's arm to move him centre stage.

'Liuetenant Byrnes has not been with us for long,' Sibley told the assembled soldiers, 'but he has shown himself to be a competent soldier and a fine officer time and time again. With Mr Slater now a major, I need a new adjutant. He is here before you now — *Captain* Byrnes.'

Unaware that he was so highly regarded by the men, Byrnes stood as cheering rocked the building. At last, waving to the troops, he went down from the stage with a feeling of pride filling him. Never in his whole life had he felt this good. He found that being a man with a purpose to be far more satisfying than life as an aimless drunk.

When he got back to his friends he

found that two other nurses had joined Cora, and Joe Higgins had returned from the hotel. All four joined Eli Whitman in complimenting him as he walked up.

'Congratulations, sir,' Whitman greeted him warmly, while an impulsive Higgins went to slap him on the back, but remembered the difference in their ranks and stopped himself.

'I am very pleased for you,' Cora said, before indicating her two female companions and adding, 'I'm afraid that I have to go.'

Byrnes said anxiously, 'Earlier I was about to ask — '

'If I would join you for dinner,' Cora finished for him. 'And I was about to say I'd be delighted to.'

'I'm so glad,' Byrnes said, taken a little out of his stride by her unhesitating response. 'Shall we say at the hotel? I'll meet you at the desk, perhaps nine o'clock?'

'That will be fine,' she agreed as she left.

Watching her go, finding a strangeness in socializing with a woman after the brutality, the noise and the terror of a battlefield, Byrnes became aware of Higgins's agitation.

'What's troubling you, Joe?' he asked as he shook the hands of several officers who were coming up to congratulate him.

Though he had denied any soldierly tendencies to everyone, and Cora Graycot in particular, he now had a real sense of belonging in the Confederate Army. After a lifetime of being looked upon as an over-privileged drunk, it was rewarding to receive such high respect.

'It's the woman at the hotel,' Higgins replied. 'I think she's the owner.'

'What about her?'

'She wants to see you, sir, in a hurry, like.'

'I don't know anyone in Santa Fe, Joe, so she must be mistaken in thinking that she knows me,' Byrnes decided.

Higgins shook his head. 'I don't

think so, sir. When I gave her your name for the register she recognized it, and said she thought she'd seen you pass by earlier.'

Mystified by this, Byrnes said, 'I'd better see what it's all about, Joe. You and Eli stay here. I'll see you both at the hotel.'

'I don't suppose there's a chance of joining you for dinner, sir?' Whitman cheekily enquired.

'If I see your ugly mug within a mile of the hotel's dining-room, Sergeant Whitman, I'll have you court-martialled,' Byrnes warned.

'That's the kind of comradeship that has me love the army, sir,' Whitman called after a departing Byrnes in mock sarcasm.

Byrnes stepped into a street alive with men in Confederate uniform. Byrnes considered how bewildering it must be for the folk of Santa Fe to see blue change to grey so swiftly. Though the senior officers were taking a break for the celebrations, preparations for the next offensive were under way. Detachments of artillery wheeled gun carriages along the streets, while victuals and ammunition were being carried from captured warehouses and loaded on to wagons. A Stars and Stripes flag lay on the street and was trampled into the dust by an infantry unit that was marching towards where the official celebrations were taking place.

Returning the salute of a two-man military police patrol, Byrnes went into the Leland Hotel. The reception area was unoccupied except for a fat-cheeked drummer who was intent on making an inventory of his case of samples, and a slightly-built Mexican clerk behind the desk. Making for the desk to ask for the hotel proprietor, a startled Byrnes heard his name called.

'Ross!'

Turning, he saw Cait Mackeever running towards him. She came into his arms, clinging to him, weeping a little, the scent of her erasing everything of his army days to take him instantly back to New York. Though taken by surprise, he held her to him.

'What are you doing here, Cait?' he eventually managed to enquire as he struggled to get things back into chronological order in his mind. This was New Mexico, not New York, and there was a war on. Cait Mackeever had no place here; she shouldn't be here.

'I followed you,' Cait replied, dabbing at her eyes with a dainty, lace-edged handkerchief. 'I made some enquiries, found out where they were taking you, sold up the Bowrey Bastille, and moved down here to buy this place.'

The extreme and unexpected change she had made left him speechless. What she had done was pointless, for tomorrow or the next day the brigade would be moving out. Fort Union in Apache Cañon, close to Glorieta, fifteen miles south-east of Santa Fe, would be the likely objective.

He warned her of this. 'I'll be gone

from here shortly, Cait.'

'I know that, Ross, but this war won't last for ever. We'll be together then.'

'But what of New York?' he asked, his mind having been programmed for an eventual return to the big city.

'New York is finished, too many restrictions there now,' she answered. 'But all that is for the future. I have another reason for wanting you here tonight, Ross. I need your help, and I know that you'll want to give it.'

'What is it?' Byrnes was intrigued but also apprehensive of anything that was likely to divert him from his new-found allegiance to the Confederate States Army.

'Come with me.'

Giving some brief instructions to her clerk, Cait turned and Byrnes followed her up a flight of stairs. They went along one landing that had doors at either side, and up another flight of stairs to a landing on the second storey. Pausing outside the door of a room,

Cait tapped lightly on it, softly called, 'It's me,' and eased the door open.

By the illumination of an oil lamp that stood on a small table in the room, Byrnes saw the blue jacket of a Union Army lieutenant hanging on the back of a chair. Stiffening, suspecting a trap though aware that Cait wouldn't be a party to such subterfuge, he unbuttoned the flap of his revolver holster.

Already inside the room, Cait turned to beckon. Taking a cautious step, Byrnes went in to see a man rising up from where he had been sitting on the bed. It took him a time, too long, to recognize the man as Kit Geogheghan.

They embraced joyfully, slapping each other on the back, the previous long years spent together instantly closing the short gap of them being apart. But despite the warmth of the reunion, there was something that wasn't quite right for Byrnes. He stepped back from Geogheghan to give himself the chance to discover what it was. Then it came to him as he saw that his friend was wearing uniform trousers that went with the jacket draped over the chair.

'Man alive, Kit!' he croaked in surprise. You're a — '

'You're right, Ross, I'm an all-fired Yankee officer,' Geogheghan acknowledged with a rueful grin.

'I let Kit hide out here when your lot came marching in, Ross,' Cait explained.

'But where does this leave us?' Byrnes asked Geogheghan, spreading his hands wide in a gesture of helplessness.

'Still the two buddies we've always been,' Geogheghan answered easily. 'We joined different sides out of necessity and by accident, not design, Ross, so it doesn't make any difference to us.'

That would have been the truth until recently. But now Byrnes had a duty towards Whitman, Higgins, all the other men who went into battle with him, and, come to that, he owed a loyalty to the Confederate States Army. His innate honesty wouldn't permit him to leave it the way Geogheghan plainly wanted him to.

'This gives me quite a problem, Kit,' he began an explanation. 'You will always be more than a brother to me, but this war calls for a much wider view of things. I've learned just what it means to serve under a flag.'

Geogheghan looked gravely at him. 'I know exactly what you're saying, Ross. I've breathed in cordite, tasted it on my lips. Friends I have made in the army have been blown to bits in front of me. Other buddies have chanced their lives to save me from a similar fate.'

'But none of this concerns either of you two,' Cait objected. 'Remember where you came from, Ross, Kit, please. You are not two opposing armies, but two buddies.'

'That's true enough, Cait, from your viewpoint,' Geogheghan conceded, 'and I guess it's the sensible view. If it was up to you and me to talk this over, Ross, we could settle this war in ten minutes.'

'But it's not up to us, Kit. I see taking you down to the compound as a prisoner, and making sure you get fair treatment, as the best thing.'

'That's not what Kit wants, Ross,' Cait said.

'No, sir,' Kit said in emphatic agreement. 'This town is ringed by pickets. What I was hoping you'd do for me, Ross, is get me out of Santa Fe so's I can rejoin my unit.'

Not replying, Byrnes put a foot up on the chair, rested an elbow on his knee and his head on his hand. Kit Geogheghan was asking too much of him. If Byrnes obliged, then tomorrow, next week, or next month, Geogheghan might pull the lanyard that sent over a shell to blow Eli, Joe and himself to smithereens. Regretting the series of events that had brought him here to meet Cait this evening, Byrnes searched his mind, his conscience, his very soul, for an excuse, a way to refuse Kit Geogheghan.

There was no solution. Too strong a link existed between Geogheghan and himself for him to be able to let his friend down. Taking his foot down from the chair, Byrnes stood upright and looked Geogheghan straight in the eye.

'If I did betray those relying on me by getting you through the cordon round Sante Fe, where would you go?'

'I know I'm asking a lot,' Geogheghan admitted humbly, 'but if you could get me half a mile out of town on the road to Glorieta, one of our patrols will pick me up.'

'But it's not too much to ask of a good friend,' Cait put in. 'The Roscoe Byrnes I know and love won't let you down, Kit.'

'If I fix you up with a Confederate uniform . . . ?' Byrnes mused.

'My lot would gun me down before I had a chance to explain,' Geogheghan, unasked, answered the question.

'Can you get Kit some civilian clothes, Cait?' Byrnes enquired.

'I've already had Miguel, my desk clerk, get these,' Cait replied, pleased with her own efficiency as she picked up a pile of Mexican clothes.

'Then get changed, Kit,' Byrnes ordered, 'and I'll get you out of town.'

'You won't regret it,' Geogheghan promised.

'I have my doubts about that,' Byrnes replied truthfully.

He was still uneasy when Cait took him and Geogheghan, wearing a Mexican outfit, downstairs. She stopped in a hall that led into the dining-room, saying, 'It's best that you go out the back door.'

Looking up at a huge clock on the dining-room wall, Byrnes saw that it was ten minutes past nine o'clock. With a shock he remembered that he was supposed to have met Cora ten minutes ago. Turning to Cait Mackeever with the intention of asking her to make his apologies to Cora, he was taken aback when Cait embraced him almost violently.

'I'm so pleased to have you back, and to find that you are the same old Ross,' she said earnestly. 'Take care, and return safely to me.'

As Cait released him, Byrnes glanced into the dining-room. Standing looking at him, dressed impeccably for their dinner appointment, was Cora Graycot. The hurt on her face wounded him deeply. Byrnes quickly turned away to head with Geogheghan for the back door of the hotel.

6

Santa Fe was quiet when Byrnes came back into town. Getting Kit Geogheghan out had taken longer than he had anticipated, and now dawn was not far off. There had been no real problem at first, as the pickets they had encountered had been disgruntled at drawing a duty on a night when their comrades were enjoying themselves. Only one had proved difficult. Suspicious of Geogheghan, whom Byrnes had passed off as a Mexican supplier of victuals to the army, the sentry had been as obstructive as a fear of Byrnes's rank would allow him to be. This had meant considerable delay, and afterwards Byrnes and Geogheghan had been put in real danger by a patrol of Federal troops who employed the tactic of shooting first and asking questions later. Before Geogheghan had managed to establish his identity, his fellow soldiers had several times come close to killing him and Byrnes.

Relieved to be back in town, hoping that there would be no repercussions to endanger the army career he now valued, he went quietly into the Leland Hotel. As far as he could tell the darkened reception area was deserted. With no idea which room had been allocated to him, the weary Byrnes was intent on finding an easy chair in which to rest until Cait Mackeever or her Mexican manager arrived to begin a new day.

As two shadowy figures suddenly loomed up from among the dark silhouettes of furniture, Byrnes snapped out of his tiredness and placed his back against the counter. Ready to defend himself, he relaxed when a voice spoke and he recognized it as that of Eli Whitman.

'Land sakes! sir, are we glad you're back,' the sergeant exclaimed. 'I've never been so worried in all my born days. A message from General Sibley came for you last thing, so me and Joe stayed down here waiting for you, sir.'

'What is it, Eli?'

'You're wanted back at camp before dawn, sir.'

'Are we moving out?' Byrnes questioned, yawning as weariness settled on him again.

'No, sir,' Higgins spoke for the first time, his voice sounding shaky. 'You've to take charge of an execution party, sir. A deserter, sir.'

Byrnes's body went icily cold so fast that he shuddered. Though it had taken him a while to be able to take a life in battle without too many qualms, this was different. Killing in combat was cloaked in anonymity, which made it easier. But this would be a harrowing case of shooting a real person in cold blood. He wouldn't be pulling the trigger, but Byrnes was aware that he would be responsible for ordering the firing squad to open up.

'I don't . . .' Byrnes began miserably, not knowing what he wanted to say.

A sympathetic Sergeant Whitman said, 'I'm sorry that this had to happen to you, sir.'

Byrnes was sorry, too. News of having been assigned this detail had completely demolished the earlier euphoria brought on by the respect of his fellow officers and his promotion. Now he bitterly regretted having come back into town. He should have persuaded Cait and Kit Geogheghan to run back to New York with him. Maybe things had changed, as Cait reported, but the three of them could have picked up at least some of the pieces.

'There's little time, sir,' Higgins respectfully pointed out. 'You'll need a shave, sir. Your room is Number 12, just at the head of the stairs. I've taken the liberty, sir, of getting your dress equipment ready, sir.'

'Thanks, Joe,' Byrnes said, gratefully but tiredly as he made his way to the stairs on leaden legs, his feet dragging.

The first shreds of daylight were streaking the eastern horizon when he was back at the camp. Fortunately, he had left the hotel before Cait Mackeever was up and around. Had they met he would have needed to confide in her. He knew Cait would share his opinion that he couldn't execute a man for doing what every soldier wanted to do at some time or other, which was run away. Cait would have made a bad situation worse, if that was possible, by persuading him to abandon this duty.

Bracing himself, Byrnes felt physically sick at the very prospect of carrying out an action for which he was totally unsuited. Unsure of what was to happen, whether he would actually have to face the soldier who was to be put to death, he asked Eli Whitman to outline the procedure. What he learned from the sergeant depressed him even more.

The army had chosen the place of execution with care. Some sort of rock quarry work in the past had produced a flat area to the rear of the camp. The quarry had been cut into a hill so that three sides were formed by a wall some forty feet high. Bushes partly closed off the remaining side. A single post had been set up close to the rear wall, facing west and the partially open side of the square. The sight of the post to which the prisoner would be tied was enough to completely defeat Byrnes's determination to remain detached from the proceedings.

His first duty was to place in position seven officials, officers ranging in rank from a first lieutenant to a lieutenant-colonel. Next he lined up twelve soldiers detailed as witnesses. Byrnes's nerve started to falter when he had Sergeant Whitman march the firing squad into position.

Aware of movement behind him, he knew that an escort had brought the prisoner up to the wide gap in the bushes. Turning slowly, Byrnes saw that the half-collapsed condemned man was supported on each side by a guard.

The prisoner's knees were refusing to hold him upright, and his hatless head was dropping. But, to Byrnes' distress, the condemned soldier raised his head. Byrnes found himself looking into the agonized, tear-stained face of Private Bristow.

Completely paralysed by this added twist of horror, Byrnes was aware of the tension stretching the surrounding silence taut. Aware that he had to march to the prisoner to lead the procession to the place of execution, he was unable to move.

'Captain Byrnes!'

A watching General Sibley had shouted his name, jerking him into action. Disturbed by a giddiness, suffering a strange, dream-like feeling of not really being there, Byrnes marched over to where Bristow and the execution party waited.

Recognizing him, the face of a weeping Bristow took on an expression of hope. He sobbed, 'Thank God you're here, Lieutenant Byrnes. You know me, sir. Please don't let them kill me!'

Filled with a despair of his own, Byrnes forced himself to turn his back on the stricken soldier. A military chaplain fell in on Byrnes' left as he led a procession made up of the prisoner, flanked on each side and supported by a guard, while immediately behind them was another guard carrying a brace-board. Bringing up the rear was the recorder, an officer a distraught Byrnes recognized as Lt Bowdler.

Halting at the post, Byrnes tried to look away into the distance as the guards tied a struggling Bristow's hands behind his back. The prisoner wailed a plea. 'Save me, save me, Lieutenant Byrnes, please.'

When Byrnes didn't respond, Bristow collapsed. The guards strapped him to the brace-board, which they brought upright and tied to the execution post. The army had overcome Bristow's physical weakness and he was now in position for the firing squad.

The command 'Attention' was given

by the recorder, and Byrnes took up his position in front of and to the right of the prisoner, while the chaplain took his position in front of and to the left of the prisoner.

'Private Bristow,' Byrnes began, surprised how steady his voice sounded, 'do you have anything to say to me before the order directing your execution is carried out?'

'Help me,' Bristow cried out loudly.

'Do you have anything to say to the chaplain?'

'Help me!' Bristow's voice rose to a scream. 'I don't want to die!'

The chaplain started to intone a prayer as he moved away. Doing a military-precise left turn, Byrnes marched over to come to a halt beside Whitman, giving a nod of his head. Sergeant Whitman's voice rang out clearly on the still air of a new day.

'Party; party ready! Take aim!'

Whitman looked to Byrnes, who, grim-faced, gave the signal.

'*Fire!*'

Rifles crackled, Bristow's body threshed about within the restraint of his bonds. Then there was an unearthly silence until the sound of the rifles echoed faintly from a far distance. There was a strong smell of cordite as, to encourage Byrnes to move, Sergeant Whitman marched towards Bristow.

Aware that all eyes, including those of General Sibley, were on him expectantly, Byrnes joined his sergeant. Bristow's body looked as if it had been run over by the spiked wheel of a carriage. It leaked blood profusely, but his head was held high, the prominent Adam's apple in his over-long neck bobbing frantically. Byrnes was disconcerted by the stare of a man who should by all logic be dead. Bristow was making low, guttural noises that resembled the sounds of a foraging pig.

Prompting Byrnes in a hissing whisper from the side of his mouth, Whitman said, 'Your pistol, sir.'

Knowing what had to be done,

Byrnes doubted that he could bring himself to do it. Lifting the flap of his holster, he drew the heavy pistol. Making machine-like, jerky movements, he pressed the muzzle against the condemned man's right temple. Bristow was looking directly into his eyes, still holding a slim hope that Byrnes would be his saviour.

'Pull the trigger, sir,' Whitman hissed secretly and urgently.

Trying to hold Bristow's gaze, Byrnes found that he couldn't. First averting his eyes, then closing them, he squeezed the trigger. The revolver barked and kicked, and he felt a splattering of something warm and moist over his hand.

Opening his eyes, he saw Bristow's bloody, shattered head had slumped to his chest. Glancing at his own hand, Byrnes's head spun and his stomach slopped around like a sea in a tempest. His hand was covered with dark-red blood and a grey/white mess of brains.

'Steady, sir, you're doing fine,' Whitman again whispered from the side of his mouth. 'End this off, sir, call the medic, then you can get away.'

Stifling a fast-rising sickness, Byrnes issued an order. This time his voice betrayed his suffering. 'Medical Officer, make your examination.'

The medical officer marched over to Bristow, made a hasty examination, then reported to Byrnes. 'Sir, I pronounce this man officially dead.'

'Medical Officer, dismiss,' Byrnes commanded before ordering the chaplain, the officials and the witnesses to fall out. He didn't look as he hurried past the guards who were cutting Bristow's body free ready to remove it. As he reached the exit through the bushes, General Sibley complimented him.

'You performed your task in a highly efficient manner, Captain Byrnes. The proceedings were conducted with dignity, solemnity and military correctness.'

'Sir,' Byrnes managed to respond to his commander before rushing off. He needed to wash and he needed to vomit. Byrnes didn't know which would come first, but both were inevitable.

Eight hours later the skin of his right hand was red raw from washing, and when he tried to be sick yet again his stomach only knotted up emptily. Yet he was just as distressed as he had been when hurrying away from the execution. Having accepted Eli Whitman's subtle invitation to join him and Higgins for a drink at the Leland Hotel, Byrnes felt it was a mistake when he sat morosely in the bar, hardly conscious of what was going on around him. A busy Cait had acknowledged his presence with a wave and a smile, but she hadn't yet been able to join him.

'A good night's sleep will help you get over it, sir,' Whitman predicted.

'Many nights will pass before I'll be able to sleep, Sergeant,' Byrnes, who couldn't shift Bristow's face from his

131

mind, replied. 'That's if I'm ever able to sleep again.'

Joe Higgins gave his support. 'I can understand that, sir. How could they make you do that to one of our own? I'd be lying if I said I ever liked Bristow, but that don't mean it didn't grieve me to see him shot down like a dog.'

'It was unpleasant, I'll grant you that,' Whitman agreed, 'but it's all part of being a soldier.'

'A soldier is something I no longer want to be,' Byrnes said firmly.

That was the truth, and he knew that he would never change his mind. Yesterday he had foolishly succumbed to praise and promotion, but he knew now that he had been fooling himself. He had no place in a system where death was handed out as casually as cigars had been distributed at the Bowery Bastille.

'You don't mean that, sir.' A worried Whitman tried to sound convincing.

'I've never been so sure of anything

in my life, Eli,' Byrnes insisted. 'I'm leaving tonight. When I get a chance to speak to Cait, I'll ask her to go with me.'

'I'd like to comment on that, sir, with your permission,' Whitman said.

Giving the sergeant a mirthless grin, Byrnes answered, 'As I am no longer a soldier, Eli, I can't be an officer either. So you don't need my permission. Go ahead, speak your mind.'

'Well,' Whitman said before pausing to choose his words. 'For a start, if you pull foot now, they'll bring you back in by tomorrow, sure as shootin'. If Cait Mackeever is with you, they won't shoot her like they will you, but she'll be given a tough time. Anyway, I don't think you've given this enough thought, sir. If Miss Mackeever ups and leaves just like that, she'll lose the investment she made in this hotel.'

It was plain to Byrnes that the sergeant was right. When Cait joined them, terribly worried about how sick Byrnes looked, he told her without going into detail that he'd had a bad experience that left him no alternative but to desert.

'But I've just found you again,' she said, close to tears. 'Where will you go, Ross?'

'I'm not sure, but I'll be back for you when the time is right,' he promised.

'I'd like to talk this over with you, Ross,' she said. 'Would your friends mind if you left them for a short while?'

'Not at all, ma'am,' Whitman smiled at her.

'The drinks are on the house, boys,' Cait told the sergeant and Higgins. 'I'll tell the barkeep as we go.'

'This is like old times, Cait,' Byrnes remarked as he followed her into her private room.

She gave him a cheeky smile. 'Not quite, we're only here to talk. Now, Ross, what's this all about?'

'I can't tell you what decided me to leave the army. I can't even stand thinking about it, so I don't want to discuss it. But I'm going, and I want you to go with me. How long would it take you to sell up?'

'No more than a couple of hours,' she replied. 'This is a little gold-mine. I get offers all the time.'

'Would you mind selling, Cait?'

'You'd be the only reason why I would' — she took hold of his hand — 'and I wouldn't hesitate if you asked.'

'It's best that you do nothing until you hear from me. Once I get back we'll head off somewhere, further west if you like, and start up something together,' Byrnes said.

'I'll be waiting, but you take care, do you hea — '

Cait broke off as there was a commotion out in the main part of the hotel. They went out of the room together to see Major Slater and a couple of junior officers shouting as they strode among the drinkers and diners.

'This is an emergency. Every man

must get back to the camp at once. Anyone not obeying within ten minutes will be deemed to have deserted. We are moving out.'

Reacting automatically, Roscoe Byrnes quickly embraced Cait and kissed her before joining the mass exodus of uniformed men. Out in the street, running towards the camp, he found Whitman and Higgins jogging at his side.

'A change of mind, sir?' an amused Whitman enquired.

Not sure what he could give as a truthful answer, Byrnes replied, 'If it's anything, Sergeant, it's no more than a postponement.'

'I'll believe you, sir,' the sergeant said, in a way that said he was lying.

'It's good to have you back, sir,' Higgins grinned at him.

'I haven't been anywhere yet, Joe,' Byrnes took a pretend swipe at the young corporal.

Turning into the camp, he came face to face with his father. Byrnes saluted the colonel while Whitman and Higgins stood stiffly to attention.

'This is the big push, Roscoe,' Rutherford Byrnes informed his son.

'We're heading for Fort Union, hopefully within the hour. Strike while the iron is hot, General Sibley says, and I agree with him. I guess you're anxious to get back in action, Son.'

'I'm not sure how I feel about anything right now, Colonel,' Byrnes replied.

'You did your duty as a soldier, Roscoe, don't take it to heart.'

'I didn't consider for one moment that my duty would involve putting a terrified boy to death,' Byrnes countered.

'The army had to make an example of that boy, Son,' Rutherford Byrnes said consolingly. 'What you had to do will discourage others from deserting. It's a case of sacrificing one man to save the lives of many.'

'I hadn't looked at it that way, Colonel.' Byrnes gave the reply he felt his father expected. In truth it seemed a cold and callous equation to him.

'We'll drink to victory when we meet again, Roscoe,' the colonel said as he walked away.

'I'll look forward to that, sir,' Roscoe called.

Hurrying on with his two companions, Byrnes wasn't sure whether he was pleased or disgusted with himself because the execution of Bristow was no longer so acutely painful in his mind.

They turned a corner where tents were being pulled down, and he saw Cora Graycot up ahead. She and the two other female nurses were loading blankets and boxes of bandages on to a wagon. Byrnes stopped beside her while Whitman and Higgins tactfully continued on their way.

'Captain Byrnes,' she greeted him politely but distantly.

'Miss Graycot.' He made a little bow. 'I wish to tender my apologies for last evening. There is no excuse for my behaviour, but in mitigation I would like to say that something unavoidable came up. A very old and dear friend was in serious trouble.'

'I saw you with her,' she nodded, an underlying annoyance in the way she slung a folded blanket up into the wagon.

'No, You are mistaken. Cait Mackeever, who owns the hotel, is indeed an old friend from New York, but it was my best buddy, Kit Geogheghan, who needed my help.'

'Whatever you say, Captain,' she answered, a little huffy still.

'Is my apology accepted, Miss Graycot?'

'Why not? I once said that I had never met an officer like you, and that still holds true. But whatever it is that sets you apart from all others, it certainly isn't that you are a liar.'

'Thank you,' he said gratefully, finding her company so enchanting that he didn't want to leave, although Cait was now occupying the sore place in his conscience that Bristow had vacated, only temporarily Byrnes was sure. 'What if in the near future I was to again ask you to have dinner with me?'

'I am not prone to bearing grudges, Captain, and it would be silly to do so in our somewhat life-threatening environment. So my answer must again be yes.'

'I am delighted and most honoured, Miss Graycot.'

'That pleases me, sir,' she smiled at him, 'but I would advise against excessively eager anticipation. It may be some time, if ever, that we return to a civilized society.'

'I pray that it won't be.'

'I hope that your prayer is answered,' she said, adding, 'Now, my gallant captain, should you not be organizing your command for what lies ahead?'

'Till we meet again.' He lifted his cap.

'May God go with you,' she said, turning away to concentrate on her work.

Byrnes hurried off in a confused state. He found Cora Graycot to be absolutely fascinating, but Cait Mackeever and Private Bristow cut through his good feelings towards the nurse, torturing his mind.

Reaching his men he snapped himself out of his bemused state by shouting, 'Right, Sergeant Whitman, Corporal Higgins, get those men moving.'

Roscoe Byrnes had returned to being a soldier.

7

Everything had gone wrong at Apache Cañon. With General Sibley called to headquarters, Colonel Byrnes was leading the Confederate Army. Rightly making a cautious approach, anticipating that this would be the first, heavily fortified outpost of the Federal defence of Fort Union, Colonel Byrnes and his army had been surprised not to have one sighting of the enemy. Like his troops, the colonel was pleased by the lack of opposition, but Major Slater, a veteran campaigner, communicated his worry to Roscoe Byrnes.

'I'm real uneasy about this, Captain Byrnes,' Slater said, going on, unusually for him, to express doubt about his commander. 'Colonel Byrnes is a mite too concerned with his own men to do much proper thinking about the Yanks.'

Byrnes tacitly agreed. Calling a halt in the pass, the colonel ordered tents to be erected and the soldiers to lay out their kit for inspection. When his dismayed officers had passed his orders on to the men, Colonel Byrnes addressed the whole battalion to explain his reasons for having taken the unusual step of enforcing discipline in a combat area.

'Most of you men have experienced fighting, some of you haven't,' the colonel said, standing on a flat rock so that every soldier could see him. 'But I am far from satisfied with our general state of preparedness. Military standards are lax. There is a sloppiness about every unit, artillery as well as infantry, that we will all have good cause to regret when we encounter the Union forces. That being so, I am going to take time to ensure that before we leave Apache Cañon for the assault on Fort Union you will have become the ultimate in disciplined and efficient fighting forces.'

'I trust this doesn't include my unit, Colonel Byrnes?' a surgeon captain enquired from where the hospital wagons had pulled in.

Byrnes looked for Cora among the hospital staff, thrilling as he caught a distant glimpse of her while listening to his father's reply. 'The discipline of your command is your concern, Captain Reid. If you are confident that you are capable of maximum efficiency, then so be it.'

'Thank you, Colonel,' Captain Reid said.

Sergeant Whitman, supervising soldiers preparing for the commander's inspection, spoke quietly to Roscoe Byrnes. 'I hate being critical of your daddy, sir, but in my experience inspections in the field are a big mistake. If we stay here any longer then the men should be digging in, not laying out their kit.'

Not having been with the military long enough to comment, Byrnes did no more than acknowledge his sergeant's misgivings with a nod. But he found the uneasiness of Whitman and other experienced soldiers to be contagious. All the officers were afraid to express their worries to the colonel because of his stern demeanour. Byrnes felt he owed it to them to make an approach, He did so, feeling ridiculous when saluting his own father.

'A lot of the men aren't happy about this inspection, Colonel,' Byrnes said.

'They are not in command, I am,' Colonel Byrnes replied tetchily.

'Nevertheless, their reaction perturbs me, sir.'

Glaring at him, then turning away to stare at a far distant range of purple hills, Colonel Byrnes spoke in a tight-lipped, angry way. 'Are you questioning my orders, Captain?'

'No. I simply wanted to express an opinion.' Byrnes dropped his military pose to speak candidly.

'Blood spilled in battle is not thicker than water, Captain,' Colonel Byrnes spoke sharply. 'Out here you are not my son, just another officer. Go back to your duties, sir.'

Rejoining his men, Byrnes unhappily informed his sergeant, 'I tried, Eli.'

'I'd have warned you had I known what you had in mind, sir,' Whitman said. 'I've known Colonel Byrnes a fair while. He only functions properly in battle or when administering discipline. There's no in between with your daddy, sir, and I'd be happier right now if the Federals had been here to engage us. That way we'd at least know what was happening.'

There was no more time for discussion because Colonel Byrnes, having decided to begin his inspection with the company his son commanded, came striding over. He was looking critically at the first soldier and his equipment, stern of face, when a whistling shriek filled the air.

A shell exploded among the tents a few hundred yards away. The roar was deafening, the earth shook, and men were blown to pieces. More shells came in like a tidal wave.

'The Yankees are hitting us with twenty-four pounder howitzers,' the knowledgeable Sergeant Whitman shouted to Byrnes above the roar of the bombardment, 'and they're coming in thick and fast.'

Instant panic had the soldiers milling around aimlessly. Officers, some of them knocked off their feet by the blast from shells exploding close by, tried to regain command of their men. But a shouted order was obeyed only until another shell ripped up the ground and blew more bodies asunder. The peculiar but distinct division of combat was taking place. Soldiers avoided moving close to the bodies that were strewn around. The superstitious mystique of death made them fear those who had, minutes ago, been close friends. Even the wounded were isolated, as if they had moved into some parallel world that the still active were forbidden to enter.

Major Slater, always cool and self-possessed under pressure, was once again the most effective officer there.

'Move your wagons back out of range, Captain Reid,' he yelled at the senior surgeon.

Anxiously watching the hospital unit move back out of the pass, Byrnes groaned inwardly as a direct hit was scored on a wagon. Jagged pieces of wood flew into the air, and two loose wheels ran in circles until colliding and falling to the ground. He wanted to dash to the rescue, but accepted that he must stay put, obey orders. Then he was filled with relief as he saw that Cora Graycot was safe. Watching her climb nimbly up into the back of a wagon, he heard Slater shout orders as the shells still came pounding in.

'Get your kit together, men, we're moving out.'

'Strike camp, Major Slater,' Colonel Byrnes shouted. 'We'll need the tents come nightfall.'

'There's no time to pull down the

148

tents, Colonel. We've lost at least thirty men so far, and that's not counting the wounded. We have to move forward to engage the enemy, sir, or we'll all die here.'

Without waiting for the colonel's permission, or even his reply, Slater began harrying Roscoe Byrnes and the other officers to get their men moving.

'Get those guns rolling, Lieutenant Bowdler,' Colonel Byrnes came up to yell at the sandy-haired artillery officer who had played an official role in the execution of Bristow. 'We are going to shell Fort Union from the four points of the compass!'

Bowdler, a keen soldier who had perfected his gunners by means of daily practice with handspike and rammer, relished the chance to move up and bombard the enemy. He was walking among the guns, hollering orders, when a shell dropped close to him. A terrific explosion followed. A cloud of thick black smoke rose, turning to dark purple as it spread. When the smoke cleared there was nothing but a hole in the ground where Bowdler had been standing.

'Captain Byrnes, take over the battery,' Slater ordered, as the foot soldiers headed off through the pass.

'I had a bad feeling about that inspection,' Whitman said as he and Byrnes got the gun carriages rolling.

'What a mess,' Joe Higgins exclaimed as he looked around at the guns and equipment that had been smashed and the bodies of soldiers who had been shattered by enemy artillery.

There had to be a Yankee artillery observer somewhere in the surrounding hills, for, as the Confederates moved forward, so did the bombardment stop. At the far end of the pass, following close on the heels of the infantry, Byrnes turned to look back. The hospital wagons had moved up and figures were tending the wounded among the wreckage of gun carriages, broken wagons and dead horses. One of them had to be Cora. Byrnes was filled with admiration for her.

It was dusk when they sighted Fort Union. With no guns firing the place had a benign look to it, making it easy to believe that it was unoccupied. But the Confederates knew that the United States troops were in there waiting. They were aware that when the battle commenced this illusion of peacefulness wouldn't even remain as a memory.

Colonel Byrnes briefed his officers. 'The infantry can bed down for the night, gentlemen. They can rest so as to be fresh for a dawn attack on the fort. Captain Byrnes, get your guns into position. You will commence firing two hours before sun-up. We'll smash as many Yankees as we can before we move in. This will be a tougher fight than Albuquerque, gentlemen, but it will be another tremendous victory for the Confederate States Army.'

As darkness fell, the plan was relayed to men who waited in that awesome time that always comes with the approach of a new night on a battlefield. As alert as ever, Eli Whitman was keeping a close eye on Fort Union. Byrnes had come to trust his judgement. The sergeant could tell where an incoming shell would land just by listening to the sound of it; some sixth sense would warn him whenever an enemy rifleman lay hidden up ahead. With a frown on his face he was in low-voiced conversation with Higgins when Byrnes walked up.

'Something bothering you again, Eli?' Byrnes enquired, trying to sound amused so as to hide his worry.

'Nothing more than a rumour, sir,' the sergeant replied. 'Something I heard back in Mesilla.'

'What was that?'

'Probably isn't worth repeating,' Whitman shrugged.

'If it's worrying you, then it's worth telling me, Eli,' Byrnes pressured his sergeant.

'Like I said, sir, there's probably nothing in it. It's just that I heard that the Colorado Volunteers would be reinforcing the garrison at Fort Union.'

Looking across to where the distant fort was faintly backlit by a gibbous moon, Byrnes remarked, 'It sure looks quiet enough right now.'

'That's what worries me, sir,' Whitman said.

'If what you've heard is true, Eli, when will we find out?' Byrnes asked.

'Once the boys attack in the morning, sir, and then — '

'It will be too late,' Byrnes finished the sergeant's sentence.

'Exactly, sir.'

Sharing Whitman's dread now, Byrnes kept his feelings concealed. 'Time will tell, Eli. Come on, and you, Joe, we'll get what sleep we can. We've an early start in the morning.'

They joined the gunners in a few hours' sleep that ended all too quickly for Byrnes. Major Slater, who never seemed to rest, came round expecting to have to awaken Byrnes a couple of hours before dawn. But Byrnes had been up and around for some time. His gunners, superbly trained by the late Lt Bowdler, worked fast and skilfully so that everything was ready when Slater arrived.

'Good work, Captain Byrnes,' Slater said.

'All ready to commence firing, Major,' Byrnes reported.

'Then go ahead,' Slater nodded. 'Let's start knocking the crap out of those Yankee scalawags.'

As the major walked away, Byrnes gave the command and the battery opened up, the noise a crescendo as it shattered the special pre-dawn silence. The bombardment had been going for an hour without any reply from the increasingly damaged fort. Byrnes was pushing the gunners to even greater effort when his father came up, something that could have been a smile pulling at the corners of his thin-lipped mouth.

'Fine show, Captain Byrnes,' the colonel congratulated him. 'You've got those damn Yankees as frightened as jack-rabbits. There'll be no fight in them when we send our infantry in.'

Byrnes looked to Eli Whitman, hoping to gauge his opinion of what the colonel had said. But the sergeant avoided eye contact. This was enough to convince Byrnes that the experienced sergeant didn't share Colonel Byrnes's confidence that an easy victory was at hand.

'Cease firing!' Byrnes shouted.

Watching the infantry head for the fort, Byrnes pitied them, especially those who were new to battle. No amount of training could prepare a soldier for the trauma of the front line. The newcomer had no idea what to expect, what to look or to listen for. Even so, it was amazing how quickly and easily a man could adapt. Although still lagging behind the likes of Whitman in experience, Byrnes, though he found it difficult to believe himself, had become a soldier virtually overnight.

He looked behind him now to see the medical wagons approaching slowly. Still a long way away, they would arrive in time to take care of the terrible casualties of war that the generals never spoke of and the public was protected from hearing about.

'The moment of truth,' Whitman said, standing at his side as the infantry, spread wide in three ranks, pressed forwards.

Whitman's truth came just moments later. It was violent, sudden and demoralizing. A rifle volley from the fort cut down most of the Confederate front rank. It looked as if the Southern army would break, but the shouted commands of officers restored order in the ranks. Though their advance had been halted, the Confederates were soon fighting back.

Colonel Byrnes came running up to his son, shouting, 'Give them support, Captain Byrnes. Open fire on the fort!'

Byrnes gave the order and his gunners recommenced firing. The shells went over the heads of the Confederate soldiers to smash into the fort. A cheer went up in the ranks of riflemen, and then the rebel yell was chorused on the morning air as they began to move forward once more, taking advantage of the havoc being wreaked by their artillery.

'Cease firing when our men are within forty yards of the fort,' Colonel Byrnes ordered.

But this order was made redundant by an unexpected happening at the fort. The gates opened and Union soldiers came pouring out, spreading wide, firing as they came. Completely overwhelmed by sheer weight of numbers, and sustaining heavy casualties, the Confederate States Army began a disorganized retreat.

Staring in dismay at what would inevitably become a defeat, Colonel Byrnes issued a command. 'Captain Byrnes, artillery is of no use to us now. Ensure that each of your gunners has a rifle, and get out there with the infantry. Tell Major Slater that he must establish and hold a line.'

'Sir,' an alarmed Higgins called to Roscoe Byrnes, pointing to the rear. 'Look!'

What must have been a full company of Federal troops was coming up on them from behind. They were approaching slowly, with the Confederate hospital wagons mixed in among them.

'They flanked us, slipped past us during the night,' Whitman muttered through clenched teeth. 'I had a feeling the Colorado Volunteers had reached the fort.'

Even from a considerable distance it could be seen that the United States soldiers were wheeling three cannon behind the main body. Halting the carriages, the Federal gunners opened fire with their cannon.

They had got the range wrong. The first shells fell short of Byrnes and the others, and Colonel Byrnes shouted an order at the Confederate gunners. 'Bring those guns about!'

With their customary smooth team-work, the gunners didn't take long to have the guns facing the rear, aimed at the advancing soldiers in blue jackets. Colonel Byrnes turned to his son.

'Commence firing, Captain Byrnes.'

'But, sir,' Roscoe Byrnes objected. 'Our doctors, nurses and the wounded are among the Federals.'

'Commence firing, Captain Byrnes,' a now angry colonel ordered. 'Our men are hard-pressed by the forces from the fort, Captain. We have to stop these troops at our rear or we'll suffer a total rout.'

'I refuse to fire on our own people, sir,' Byrnes, watched anxiously by Whitman and Higgins, firmly told his father.

'You are a soldier, sir,' Colonel Byrnes fumed, 'and you will obey orders.'

The Federals fired again, the shells landing closer this time, while their infantry continued to advance, using the Confederate hospital unit and wounded as a shield.

'Commence firing!' Colonel Byrnes yelled at Whitman.

But the sergeant's only reaction was to look to Roscoe Byrnes for his order. Byrnes could now discern the Confederate wagons among the sea of Union uniforms. Artillery shells were not selective. There was no way of killing Yanks while leaving the Southern units unharmed.

His father had calmed down. It could be that he was empathizing with his son. The colonel said in a reasonable tone, 'This is war, Captain Byrnes, and a military commander has to carry out actions that in normal times he would regard as repulsively obscene. We are vastly outnumbered and cannot possibly fight on two fronts. Whatever the price our consciences have to pay, those columns advancing to our rear have to be halted.'

Accepting this as an accurate assessment of the situation, Roscoe Byrnes agonized. He deplored the foolishness that had made him return to the army after presiding over the execution of Bristow. Continuing as an officer hadn't enabled him to escape from the conviction that he had murdered the young soldier. Now he was being forced to kill the courageous Cora Graycot, who had become very special to him. Others, too, would die. Young soldiers already suffering from wounds would be slain by supposedly friendly guns.

Yet there was no alternative. The troops from the fort were steadily driving the Confederates back. Most of them would die if Federal troops were allowed to attack them from behind as well.

Without looking out to where the Union soldiers and the Confederate hospital wagons were moving closer, he gruffly ordered Whitman: 'Commence firing, Sergeant.'

A soldier to the core, Whitman responded instantly to the command by shouting orders to the gunners.

Cait Mackeever came into Byrnes's mind as he forced himself to look at the slowly approaching columns. Though she was necessarily tough when running her business in New York, the innately kind and caring Cait would be aghast if she knew what he was about to do. Realizing this brought home to Byrnes how the army had changed him. Though the Roscoe Byrnes in New York hadn't amounted to much, nothing would have induced him to kill innocent people. Innocent people, including a woman for whom he had strong feelings.

Coming to a decision, having no regard for the consequences that would follow cancelling the firing of the guns, he shouted to Whitman, 'Hold it, Sergeant.'

'What are you doing, Roscoe?' his father cried, forgetting army rank and protocol in his anguish.

Sergeant Whitman, the guns ready to fire, waited, his eyes on Byrnes, who

162

was shaking his head and starting to say, 'We can't fire on our own — '

His sentence was cut off by several things happening at once, suddenly and explosively. The approaching Union cannon got the range at last. Shells exploded all around them. Byrnes saw one of his guns blown on to its side, trapping a screaming gunner beneath it. Two other gunners collapsed, folding and merging into the ground the way the dead do. More shells came whistling in. Byrnes saw the shock on his father's face, and for a moment he regretted cancelling the order to open fire. Had he not done so then the gunners already dead would be alive, and those sure to die in the continuing bombardment would be saved.

But even worse things were taking place. The Confederate assault force that had been turned into a fragile defence by Federal soldiers from Fort Union, disintegrated under the ferocity of an attack by an enemy which outnumbered them by something like four to one.

Being cut down as they ran, the Confederate soldiers headed back to where they had started out, the Federal troops following at a deliberately planned distance. This was when the Union guns at the fort opened up for the first time. The barrage smashed into the running soldiers, turning a retreat into carnage. The guns targeting Byrnes kept up a continuous fire, causing death and destruction.

In what had become a hopeless situation, Byrnes saw his father running towards the retreating soldiers, holding up both hands as if he expected this would stop the retreat. As an exploding shell knocked out yet another of Byrnes's guns, Sergeant Whitman came to him out of the smoke. The gunners who remained alive and uninjured were running away without any destination in mind. Their main object was to escape from the heavy bombardment.

The Federal columns were close now, and Byrnes could see that the infantry had taken their rifles from their shoulders and were holding them ready to attack. In the direction of the fort, droves of Confederate soldiers were abandoning their arms and surrendering. The capture of Fort Union, a vital factor in the Confederates' strategy, had failed. It seemed to Byrnes that the Civil War in New Mexico was all but over.

'This is the end, sir,' Whitman shouted above the crashing explosions. 'All we can do is attempt to save ourselves. If we move before the Yankees reach here, we might get away.'

The loyal Joe Higgins joined the sergeant. Carrying two rifles, Higgins tossed one to Byrnes, who caught it.

'We'll need these, sir,' Higgins said, holding up his rifle to indicate what he meant.

'I guess we will. Thanks, Joe.'

'It's time to go, sir,' Whitman hollered.

'I'll follow you, Eli,' Byrnes yelled back, his shame at running balanced out by relief at being saved from firing on his own people.

8

Their dirty, torn uniforms meant that Byrnes, Whitman and Higgins entered the small town unnoticed. The streets were filled with other fugitives from a close to defeated army. Discipline was non-existent. Some of the men were maimed and disfigured by ugly, untreated wounds. Many were unshod, hobbling on sore, blistered feet that had trodden rough trails for too long. These were the 'lucky' ones, the Confederates who had fled from the battle at Fort Union where hundreds of their comrades had been captured or killed. They spoke excitedly about 'going home', but it was talk made empty by knowledge that their former homes were in ruins and could offer them nothing but poverty. In an atmosphere of despair the men drank to excess and wildly caroused, bullying and terrorizing the helpless civilian inhabitants.

'This is about all that remains of General Sibley's drive to the Pacific, sir,' Whitman remarked bitterly, looking around as the three of them ate a meal of kale leaves and bacon in a dingy eating-house.

It amused Byrnes that the sergeant's rigid military code still pertained. They had covered hundreds of miles on foot over countless days, and had slept, cold and hungry, under the stars for as many nights, yet Whitman still called him 'sir'.

'It all ended just as I was getting to like being a corporal,' Joe Higgins grumbled wryly.

'And you were becoming accustomed to being a captain, eh, sir?' the sergeant asked Byrnes.

'I don't rightly think that's so, Eli,' Byrnes disagreed.

Although at times the army had held an appeal for him, especially on occasions when things were going

168

right, the fact that he once found himself liking the life now seemed ridiculous. Not having chosen to be in the army, he had never properly been a soldier. No real officer would have wilfully disobeyed an order as he had. Although still glad that he hadn't given the order to fire — an order that would have put Cora Graycot's life in jeopardy — he recognized his refusal had probably contributed to the total rout of Confederate troops. Even more distressing was the likelihood that he was responsible for the death of his father.

This possibility hadn't affected him as it should due to his worry over Cora Graycot. Her beauty put her at risk as the only attractive young woman among men made dangerously unstable by war.

'What have you planned for the future, Eli?' Byrnes enquired as a diversion from his gloomy thinking.

Shrugging his broad shoulders, the sergeant replied, 'Nothing definite to speak of, sir, I guess I'll just drift further south and find myself another war.'

'And you, Joe?'

'I ain't really thought about it, sir,' Higgins confessed. 'The way I hear tell of things, there don't seem much point in going home. I suppose, if Sergeant Whitman will have me, I might as well mosey down south, too.'

'I'll be pleased to have you along, Joe,' Whitman assured the younger man, before asking Byrnes, 'Is there any chance of you joining us, sir?'

With a negative shake of his head, Byrnes answered, 'I reckon my soldiering days are just about done, Eli. I'll head back to Santa Fe and collect Cait, then we'll return to New York.'

Put into words, that sounded like an attractive prospect, but Cora loomed too large in his mind for Byrnes to fully accept the idea. Yet he knew he had to be realistic. Cora would now be a captive of the Federals as a prisoner. The chance of their trails ever again crossing was an extremely remote one. Life had ceased to be uncomplicated from the moment he had been forcibly removed from the carefree environment of the New York drinking dens. Maybe if Cait, Kit Geogheghan and he were back in Gotham they could pick up the pieces and carry on as if they'd never left.

Voices raised in excitement out on the street broke into their conversation. They stood, Byrnes tossing some coins on to the table before following his two companions outside. A crowd of men in soiled grey uniforms, technically military deserters but in reality the remnants of a shattered army, were looking west to where a column of troops was making a snake-like approach to the town.

'Seemed to me at first that they were Union troops,' a bearded soldier commented. 'But them boys are wearing the same colour as us. They're Confederates, men.'

Byrnes could see some gun carriages

being pulled along. Something useful had survived the disastrous assault on Fort Union. But there weren't enough armaments there to fight another serious battle. The soldiers looked worn out, approaching in a shambling walk rather than a march. Even the mounted officers and their horses had an appearance of exhaustion.

'I hate to offer bad tidings, sir,' Whitman said quietly to Byrnes, 'but seems like you're going to have to put off your visit to Santa Fe. If my tired eyes aren't deceiving me, that's either the ghost of your daddy or the colonel himself riding alongside General Sibley.'

Realizing that the sergeant was right, Byrnes experienced conflicting emotions of which he wasn't proud. Though he had been hoping that his father was safe, the colonel's survival ended Roscoe Byrnes's brief freedom from the Confederate States Army. His only chance was to escape now. He heard the pointlessness of such a move spoken of by two soldiers who were standing close by.

'If we don't pull foot right away, Hector,' a boy of about seventeen years of age remarked, 'we're going to find ourselves back in line, with them Yankees blasting our asses off.'

'You're dad-blamed correct there, Sam, but there just ain't no place to run to,' the boy's older companion said hopelessly.

The column reached the edge of town. With no alternative, Byrnes and his two friends walked to meet it. His father, General Sibley and Major Slater, who were riding at the front, reined up as Byrnes saluted them smartly.

'I'm pleased that you are safe. Captain,' Sibley said, 'both for the sake of your father and the army. We need every good man.' Rising up a little in his stirrups, he viewed the disorganized groups of undisciplined men standing around in the town. 'It is our responsibility to turn this rabble back into a fighting force. We are to make for the Rio Grande and re-engage the enemy there.'

Seeing the shocked disbelief this brought to the faces of Byrnes, Whitman and Higgins, Colonel Byrnes, who had shown no reaction to having discovered his son to be safe and well, spoke up to give a military-style report.

'On the morrow we shall be reinforced by eight hundred Texans who are bringing up supply wagons.'

Maybe the supplies would be useful, but Roscoe Byrnes didn't feel that just 800 men would be of much help against the undoubted might of the Union army. Neither did being part of a team trying to shape the rabble in town back into a fighting force appeal to him. It was then he learned from Major Slater that Sibley had other plans for him.

'I want you to prepare immediately for an important mission, Captain Byrnes,' the coldly efficient major said. 'The Federals are at this time encamped at Canoncito, where we will be heading once we have reorganized our army here.'

'But I don't intend to engage the enemy before we regain our medical team,' General Sibley took over from Slater. 'We want you to command a small party to return our surgeons and their wagons to us. Select as many men as you need, Captain, the choice is yours. All I insist upon is that you make haste.'

'I request that Sergeant Whitman and Corporal Higgins accompany me, sir.'

It had just dawned on Roscoe that this rescue patrol would reunite him with Cora. What had struck him as an unpleasant and hazardous duty was fast becoming an attractive prospect. Having his two stalwart friends with him increased the chances of success for the mission.

'Very well,' Major Slater replied on behalf of the general. 'What number of men will you take with you, Captain?'

'No more than three in addition

to us, sir,' Roscoe answered. With a small command he could move fast and unnoticed. He was aware of Whitman's approving eyes on him. The military-minded sergeant was pleased to note that Byrnes was learning fast.

An hour later, General Sibley had set up his headquarters in a large woodworking shop. A former Yankee sutler's store had been assigned to Byrnes for him to prepare his rescue mission. It was there that an apologetic Whitman returned after Byrnes had sent him out with Higgins to find three good men. With Whitman and Higgins was a trio of part-uniformed ruffians.

Byrnes left Higgins in charge of the new men and took Whitman to one side. Before he could question the sergeant, Whitman swiftly explained.

'These three's the best of a real poor lot, sir. I've known all of them at one time or another, and the only thing I'm certain of is that they were once good soldiers.'

'Indeed,' a dubious Byrnes said.

'That fella with the beard is Oscar Symington, sir.'

A black beard and an unwashed face made Symington as dark as a Negro. His eyes, one of which bulged grotesquely, were startlingly white. Bright with what Byrnes interpreted as madness, the odd-matched eyes glared continuously at him. The man had a lean, gangling build that, though deceptively awkward, was that of a formidable fighting man.

'Symington was a lieutenant when I knew him, sir,' Whitman was continuing. 'Got busted back to the ranks down close to El Paso. That wasn't anything to do with soldiering, sir. They say Oscar lost his head over some Texas woman.'

'There won't be any women to distract him where we're going, Eli,' Byrnes remarked, accepting Whitman's first choice with a nod, then turning his attention to a fat young man with incredibly short legs. 'Can that guy sit a horse, Eli?'

'Don't be fooled by how Billy Strachey looks, sir,' Whitmore advised. 'Billy's meaner than all get-out. Needs watching though, because once the enemy's been seen off, Billy's got to be stopped from killing those on his own side. The third fella's Art Greenham. Looks like he's more'n half asleep, don't it, sir? But you'll find that Art's awake when he's needed in a fight. I've soldiered with him, sir. Like the other two, he's unpredictable, but you couldn't have a better man at your side on the battlefield.'

Studying the unwholesome trio for a while, Byrnes made himself a promise. Rescuing Cora Graycot would be his final mission for the Confederate States Army. He would leave immediately afterwards. Where he would go and what he would do initially depended on Cora. Assuming that he got her back safe and well — an overly optimistic assumption — he would ask her to ride with him. Though he would regret abandoning Cait, he would take solace in the knowledge that the fiery Miss Mackeever was well capable of taking care of herself.

Walking over to face the three men, Byrnes wasn't saluted by any of them. Greenham, his heavy eyelids drooping, didn't seem to notice Byrnes's presence. With the fat round face and pouting lips of a baby, Strachey acknowledged him with a barely perceptible nod. Symington continued his fierce glare, lips moving like he was silently putting a curse on Byrnes.

'You men have been selected for a special mission,' Byrnes began. 'We're moving out at first light, heading down Canoncito way.'

Symington gave a vehement shake of his head of greying, uncombed hair. When he spoke, his voice was surprisingly deep and resonant for a narrow-chested man. 'I won't be going with you, mister. All I'm interested in is collecting the *dinero* that's long due to me, and heading off in whatever direction I choose.'

179

'I'm not *asking* you, Soldier, I'm *telling* you,' Byrnes said harshly. 'You should recognize an order when you hear it. Sergeant Whitman tells me that you were an officer at one time.'

'I won't deny that, *mi amigo*, but that was in a real outfit. This isn't an army any more. We've had our asses whupped real good.'

'That sure is true,' Strachey supported Symington's bitterly expressed opinion.

'Who gave you permission to speak, Soldier?' Whitman put his face close to that of Strachey to hiss his question.

A defiant Strachey locked eyes with the sergeant. 'I don't need no permission because I'm all through. I quit this goddamn army when them Yankees chased us away from Fort Union.'

'Looks to me like you got your answer,' Symington said with a mirthless grin at Byrnes. 'Me'n Billy's just about to walk out on you. You've still got Greenham, but probably only until he wakes up.'

'Stand still!'

Byrnes's shout halted Symington and Strachey as they were walking towards the door. When the two men turned, both Whitman and Higgins were holding rifles at hip level, covering them.

'You have your orders, men,' a stern Byrnes told them. 'You'll report here at sun-up, ready to ride out. Failure to do so will mean you being rounded up and shot, at once and without trial.'

As lithe and noiselessly as a mountain cat, Symington walked up to face Byrnes. He kept his voice low, but all present heard his chilling words. 'You are making a big mistake. It's not us who will die, *compadre*. You have just passed a sentence of death upon yourself. I will kill you. Perhaps tonight, maybe tomorrow when we are away from here, or possibly it will be the next day. Whenever, *mi amigo*; I will kill you some time. You can be sure of that.'

'You just be sure you're here at dawn, and you, Strachey,' Byrnes said, turning his head to where an uninterested Greenham stood. 'What about you, Soldier, have you got a beef?'

'Well now,' Greenham drawled, shrugging and partly raising just one eyelid. 'Seems to me as how I'll get shot if I stay here, and shot if I goes with you. I reckon as how I'd like to enjoy a little ride before I fetches a bullet in the brisket, so I guess I'll be going along with you.'

'Then be here at first light,' Byrnes reminded him, adding, 'And say 'sir' when you address me.'

'Yes, sir,' Greenham sleepily obliged.

When the three of them had left, Whitman and Higgins stood dutifully waiting for Byrnes to decide what he wanted them to do. Appreciating their unswerving loyalty, and what they had been through, he wanted them to relax and have some fun before the perilous mission began. But a worried Whitman had a warning for him.

'Oscar Symington meant what he said, sir.'

'I didn't doubt that for a moment, Eli.'

'We'll be looking out for you, sir, along the way. Me'n Joe will be watching your back.'

'I'm grateful to both of you. Now, you boys take the rest of the night off,' Byrnes told them. 'Enjoy yourselves, but go easy on the liquor. I want you both with clear heads and fighting fit in the morning.'

'You can depend on us, sir,' Higgins assured him.

'You don't need to tell me that, Joe.'

'What about you, sir? Will you come with us?' Whitman hopefully enquired.

'I'd sure like to, Eli,' Byrnes smiled, 'but I've to head down to HQ to go over maps of the territory with Major Slater. I'll see you both at sun-up.'

'We'll be here before that, sir,' Whitman said, coming smartly to attention.

9

Leaving town as the sun rose, they rode through gold-tipped hills. Crossing rocky terrain, taking meandering trails through woods they came to open prairie. Symington, Strachey and Greenham remained aloof but gave no trouble. In the cool of evening with the horses tiring and the riders weary, they came across an isolated cabin.

'Looks like some kind of relay station, sir,' Whitman observed.

'It would suit us fine for the night,' Byrnes said, using a neckerchief to wipe thick dust from his face. 'I'd say it was unoccupied, but check it out, Sergeant.'

Dismounting, Whitman, rifle held in front of him, cautiously approached the old log cabin. Remaining in the saddle, an alert Joe Higgins used his rifle to cover his friend.

When Whitman gave the all-clear signal, Byrnes and the others dismounted and moved in. The cabin was old and in many places the clay chinking between the logs had fallen out, making fine loopholes.

Indicating these, Whitman said, 'If we should get trouble, sir, those holes will come in mighty handy.'

'I don't anticipate any shooting, Eli,' Byrnes replied.

Whitman had Strachey take care of the horses. He sent Symington and Greenham out into the thick, close to impenetrable, undergrowth of willows to collect wood for the rusty stove. The two men returned grinning, bringing with them wild plums and grapes plucked from vines that were strung about like strands of wire.

'We ain't going to be fit to take on the Yankees if we're all doubled up with the belly-ache, sir,' Strachey laughed, as in an astonishingly convivial atmosphere they eagerly sampled the fruit.

'What will we be facing up ahead,

sir?' Greenham asked.

'I can't say for sure, Greenham,' Byrnes admitted. 'We've to rescue our surgeons' team, but nobody knows the strength of the States force holding them captive.'

'That don't sound like no well-planned campaign to me, sir,' Greenham said laconically.

'What do you expect?' Strachey grumbled. 'This is the Confederate States Army.'

Whitman, Higgins and Greenham laughed at this pessimistic view. Only Symington remained outside of the friendly circle. Retaining his morose, smoulderingly threatening attitude, his cold gaze never strayed far from Byrnes.

When they had eaten and slaked their dust-induced thirst with countless cups of coffee, Whitman arranged guard duties for the night.

'All that's required is one man on look-out on that small rise yonder,' the sergeant said. 'We'll split it up into spells of two hours. Corporal Higgins, you go first, from nine o'clock till eleven. Then you, Symington, with Strachey next, Greenham following him, and then I'll take over.'

Able to relax with Higgins on watch, Byrnes got into his blankets. Determined to sleep only until it was Symington's time to take over guard duty, he underestimated his tiredness. A kick in the ribs awakened him. In the meagre moonlight filtering through the cabin's one window, he saw Higgins lying in blankets. He had slept longer than he intended. Something had gone very wrong.

'There's no use in reaching for your gun, Captain, we've got that,' Byrnes heard Symington's voice say.

Symington was standing over Byrnes, pointing a rifle down at him. Greenham and Strachey had Whitman and Higgins covered.

'We want no part of this shindig you got planned, Byrnes,' Symington went on. 'Me and the boys are riding out.

But I won't leave any of you out here unarmed. Give us time to get away, and you'll find your weapons in the brush where the river forks, about three miles due south.'

'You're making a mistake, Symington,' Byrnes warned.

'Maybe,' Symington nonchalantly answered as the three of them went out the door.

'We heading out after them, sir?' Whitman asked eagerly, as Byrnes stood and fixed his bedroll.

'Best give them a little time, Eli,' Byrnes advised. 'Us being unarmed won't make any difference to Symington. If we come up behind him too soon he'll blast us out of our saddles.'

Ready to leave within minutes but frustrated by the need to delay, they were pacing the small cabin when the drumming of hoofs made them hurry to the one window.

'They're back!' Whitman exclaimed in puzzlement.

Looking out, Byrnes assumed that

Symington and his two companions were being chased. He shouted to Higgins, 'Open the door, Joe.'

Skidding their mounts to a halt, Symington, Greenham, and Strachey dismounted while still on the move. As Higgins swung open the door they charged in. Breathing heavily, they carried their own weapons and those they had confiscated from the others. Once inside they tossed Whitman and Higgins their rifles, and Byrnes caught his revolver as Symington sent it spinning through the air.

'There's a bunch of renegades on our tail,' Strachey informed them.

'Guerrillas,' Symington qualified Strachey's statement. 'A bunch of Union runaways by the look of them.'

'How many?' Byrnes asked tersely.

'Ten — twelve at the most.'

Byrnes questioned Symington sharply. 'How far are they behind you?'

'Too close. They'll be here within minutes.'

Rapidly assessing the situation, Byrnes

issued orders. 'Eli, you, Higgins, Strachey and Greenham, find yourselves vantage points to defend the cabin from the inside. Those holes of yours will serve you well now, Eli. Symington, you and me are going outside.'

'I'd rather stay in here and take my chances,' Symington objected.

Aware that if they all remained inside the guerrillas would have them trapped, Byrnes took a threatening step towards Symington. Their sole strategy was to have the two of them concealed in the brush behind the cabin. From there they would watch and wait to spring a surprise.

'Quit arguing and get moving,' Byrnes ordered Symington.

They went out through the door, hurrying round to the back of the cabin. There was no sound of hoofbeats, but the instinctive feel for danger that had developed in Byrnes since he'd come out West told him that the guerrillas had left their horses and were coming forward on foot.

Crouching with Symington at his side in the dense undergrowth with a good view of the approach to the cabin, Byrnes watched and waited. A sense of dread churned in him. Should he fail in this unexpected encounter with Union guerrillas, then the Confederate surgeons' detachment and, more importantly to him, Cora Graycot, would be lost, most probably for ever.

A heavy New York-accented call broke into his thoughts.

'You men in the shack,' came the shout. 'We mean you no harm. Like you we are soldiers; like you, we're sick of war. We are all pals together now, so join us.'

If genuine, this was an invitation to become part of a lawless band committing robbery and murder. Someone in the cabin replied with a rifle shot.

The response was a volley of rifle fire that ripped and tore at the wooden structure. Counting the return fire carefully, Byrnes was satisfied that no one in the cabin had been hit. A nudge from Symington's elbow drew his attention to a figure in a blue tunic moving stealthily through the willows to their right, seeking a position to fire through the cabin window.

As Symington brought his rifle up, Byrnes reached out a hand to stay him. It was a dilemma. The Federal runaway was a real threat to those inside the cabin, but if Symington fired at him it would betray their position. Reaching a decision, Byrnes silently instructed Symington not to fire.

Anxiously watching the guerrilla, Byrnes caught a movement from the corner of his eye. He saw Symington reaching behind his neck with his right hand. The hand came back holding a knife. Symington held the tip of the knife blade between a thumb and forefinger and sent it speeding through the air.

The blade went into the guerrilla's chest from the side, burying itself to the hilt. A rush of air made a gurgling escape from the renegade's lungs as he collapsed sideways. One minor spasm shook the prone body as the man died.

Relief was diluted for Byrnes by proof of how dangerous Symington was. But there was no time to dwell on such things. He gestured to Symington, indicating a course through the brush that would keep them concealed while moving forward.

Together, made unlikely companions by necessity, Byrnes and Symington crawled through the resisting, scratching tumbleweed to reach a position behind the Union men. Just as they got there a bullet from the cabin hit one of the guerrillas in the shoulder. Maddened by pain, the man automatically stood upright to run, and a second bullet tore the top of his skull away.

Byrnes made a quick count: eight left. No direct attack would succeed against so many. Swiftly devising a plan, with a puzzled Symington following him, he crawled away.

An angry Symington reached his side to ask, 'Are you figuring on abandoning the others, Byrnes?'

'No, that's the way you operate, Symington, not me,' Byrnes retorted. 'Those men have left their horses back here somewhere.'

Not being a slow thinker, Symington grasped what Byrnes's plan was. Well clear of the guerrillas, they stood and hurried to where ten saddled horses stood hitched to trees. As they got up on what looked to be the best two mounts, Byrnes said, 'We'll drive the other horses before us and go in shooting.'

'Hold on a minute, Byrnes,' the doubting Symington protested. 'That'll put us right in the line of fire from the cabin when we go in.'

'Start hollering as soon as we get close,' Byrnes said. 'That way they'll hear us in the cabin. Sergeant Whitman will realize what's happening and stop firing.'

'I sure hope you're right, *mi amigo*,'

Symington muttered.

Pushing the horses in front of them, they headed back the way they had come. The sharp slope of the ground and density of the undergrowth made it tough going, but they were able to keep the horses on course. Biding his time as the gunfire up ahead grew louder, Byrnes finally shouted at Symington, 'Now!'

Giving the rebel yell they panicked the horses in front of them into a gallop. Keeping up close, they saw the guerrillas frantically trying to scramble out of the way. Most of them made it, but Byrnes saw the bodies of two trampled under flailing hoofs that horribly mashed their heads.

Firing from the saddle, he brought two more down, and saw Symington's rifle claim a pair of them in quick succession. Before those in the cabin realized what was happening and had ceased firing, three of the galloping horses had been slaughtered. A guerrilla trying to flee died as his throat was torn open by a bullet.

Only one man remained, and Byrnes was aiming at him when disaster struck. The rifle fire from the cabin had stopped, but the free horses, eyes crazy with fear, froth blowing whitely from their open mouths, wheeled about and came charging back. One of them collided heavily with Byrnes's mount, coming close to unseating him. He saw another unsettle Symington, who recovered swiftly to concentrate on the remaining guerrilla.

But Symington had been distracted for too long. The Yankee, a stout man approaching middle-age, adopted a firm stance to bring his rifle up. Still unable to get back into the action, Byrnes admired Symington's reflexes as he pulled hard on the reins and his horse reared up on to its back legs to act as a shield for him as the guerrilla pulled the trigger.

The bullet shattered the jaw of Symington's horse, coming out of the top of its head like a huge red plume worn for decoration. Symington scrambled clear to land flat on his back, losing his rifle as the horse fell sideways. Stooping quickly to pick up the rifle, the guerrilla threw it into the brush before swinging his body round to press the muzzle of his rifle against Symington's forehead.

Down off his horse now, Byrnes levelled his revolver at the guerrilla's back. With no interest in saving Symington, Byrnes squeezed the trigger and the Yankee threw up both arms, releasing his rifle unfired as he fell dead.

Revolver still in his hand, Byrnes walked over to look down at the unarmed Symington. With the guerrillas taken care of it would solve Byrnes's last problem if he killed the man who had become his bitter enemy. Symington's hand was going to the back of his neck before he remembered that his knife was still buried in the chest of a guerrilla. Lowering his arm, he looked defiantly up at Byrnes.

'Go ahead then, shoot me, Byrnes. I'm not afraid to die. All I ask is that you do it quickly and surely.'

Holding Symington's steady gaze, Byrnes aimed the revolver at a point between his eyes, squinting down the sights. Finger tensing round the trigger, Byrnes recognized that Symington was a split second from death, and in less time than that he would become a murderer. Easing the hammer back down, he lowered the gun, becoming aware of the sweat on his brow as the air turned it cold.

'I hope I don't live to regret this, Symington,' he said softly.

'I hope you don't,' a grinning Symington remarked ambiguously.

Unspeaking, they made their way down to the cabin. Strachey was the only casualty in the fight, and his injury wasn't serious. A sliver of wood sliced from the cabin wall had cut his ear. It was a minor injury but the blood flowed copiously.

'Ears always do pump out the red stuff,' a sleepy Greenham said as he pressed a pad against the damaged ear and wrapped a bandanna round Strachey's head.

When this was completed, Byrnes gave the order to saddle up. The skirmish with the guerrillas had cost them time. With the next battle between General Sibley and the Union Army scheduled to take place near the Rio Grande, the Federals holding the Confederate medical team would be moving that way. It would be too late to save Cora and the others if their captors joined up with the main force.

'We're heading south for Canoncito,' Byrnes called as they climbed up into the saddle.

Byrnes set a steadier pace than before. He wanted the horses to have energy in reserve in case the ride led straight into a fight. In the lead with Whitman, he had Higgins riding behind him. Symington, who had been behaving furtively since they'd left the cabin, was bunched up with Strachey and Greenham further back. Uneasy about this, Byrnes was turning in the saddle to order Higgins to drop back and bring up the rear, only to discover he was too late.

They were passing a dense wood on their left. At sign from Symington, Strachey and Greenham joined him in a dash for the trees. The alert Whitman had his rifle unsheathed and up to his shoulder.

'Shall I get Symington, sir?' he asked.

Once among the trees the escapees would be impossible to find. All three were already lost to Byrnes, and killing Symington would make no difference.

'No, Eli, let them go.'

Lowering his rifle, Whitman shrugged. 'I guess they weren't a lot of use to us, sir.'

'Up on the hill by the cabin, I came

within an inch of killing Symington, Eli.'

'You should have done it, sir.'

'He was unarmed,' Byrnes explained.

'Symington wouldn't have let that stop him if it was you who was unarmed, sir,' Higgins, who had ridden up level to them, remarked.

'Probably not, Joe,' Byrnes agreed.

'It would have ended up the same no matter who we brought with us, sir,' Whitman said. 'All the fight's been knocked out of our boys. They just aren't interested any more.'

'You're saying the Confederate States are beaten, Eli?'

'It's all over bar the white flag being waved, sir,' Whitman replied unhappily. 'Nevertheless, we'd better get moving.'

As Whitman and Higgins moved their horses forward, Byrnes spurred his mount to move ahead of them. Pulling his horse around, he faced the two soldiers, blocking their path.

'The trouble is, boys,' he said, 'I

don't know what sort of odds we'll be facing.'

'There's sure going to be more than three of them,' a gloomy Higgins predicted.

'Exactly,' Byrnes acknowledged with a nod. 'That's the point I want to make. We'll take a vote on this to decide whether we go on or go back.'

'Can I ask what you would elect to do, sir?' Whitman enquired.

'That goes without saying, Eli.'

'Those are my sentiments, too, sir,' Whitman said, permitting himself a grin as he turned to Higgins. 'Looks like you've been out-voted, Joe.'

Higgins gave a shake of his head. 'Not so, Eli. Soon's the captain spoke I gave it some thought. Sure, we don't know what's up ahead, but we do know what's back there — nothing. My vote would have been to press on.'

'I really appreciate your support, Eli, Joe.'

'It's well deserved, sir,' Whitman said. 'You could right now vote to go back to New York, and no one would stop you.'

'Maybe when we get where we're going you'll both have reason to wish I had chosen New York,' Byrnes warned.

10

They spotted the Federal horseman some five miles out of Canoncito. Riding in a rough triangle formed by a towering bluff to the south, and the erratic river that swung away in a double curve before returning to the bluff, the Yankee had to come their way. They waited on horseback just inside a narrow ravine.

'He's riding like he's all alone in this world, sir,' Joe Higgins observed.

'I figure there's more to it than that,' Whitman said quietly.

Byrnes silently agreed. Holding the reins with his left hand, the rider was clutching at his midriff with his right. The horse was doing little more than a walk, too slow for a man alone at so dangerous a time.

'Looks to me like he's hurt,' Byrnes said.

Judging his nearness by the steady clip-clop of the mount's hoofs, they moved out to confront the Union soldier.

His blue tunic was soaked in blood. He offered no opposition as Higgins reached for the bridle and halted his horse.

The soldier was young, his face ashen. His blue eyes were lent a startling brilliance by pain. His voice was faint.

'Do what you will,' he said resignedly.

'You've nothing to fear from us, Soldier,' Byrnes promised. 'We'll tend your wound.'

'No!' The Federal man's one word was startlingly loud. Then his voice faded. 'I'm done for. I want to die in the saddle.'

'Who shot you, Soldier?' Byrnes asked. There were no Confederates in the region other than his two companions and himself.

Haltingly, the injured man explained they had been jumped at Canoncito by a bunch of guerrillas. Fourteen of the company had been killed. Only twenty Union soldiers had survived.

'You holding Confederate prisoners in Canoncito, Soldier?' Byrnes enquired tersely.

The rider answered hoarsely. 'Yes, a bunch of medics and women. We were heading for Peralta where General Canby's waiting. He's been joined there by the Colorado Volunteers.'

This was bad news. The Union Army would be of formidable strength at the coming battle. The Union soldier went on, 'I'm riding to Peralta to get help.'

'You're going the wrong way, Soldier,' Byrnes advised.

'What difference does it make?' the Yankee said philosophically. 'I'd never get there. I sure hope Major Geogheghan can make it to Peralta.'

'What name was that?' Byrnes questioned sharply.

'Major Kit Geogheghan. Best danged officer ever.'

'He's in command at Canoncito?' Byrnes couldn't credit this stroke of luck.

'Yes,' the Yankee replied with his last breath. He fell sideways, only his feet being trapped in the stirrups holding him on the back of the horse.

'Get him down and bury him,' Byrnes ordered.

Whitman and Higgins laid the rider on the ground while they scraped a shallow grave. Searching through the dead man's pockets, Byrnes found his army documents and some personal letters. Whitman lifted the body by the shoulders, Higgins took the feet, and they laid him in the grave.

' 'Man that is born of woman is of few days and full of trouble',' Higgins intoned, adding after an apologetic shrug, 'I don't know the rest.'

'That will do, Joe,' Byrnes said as Higgins and Whitman started to cover the body.

'Do we make camp here, sir?' Whitman enquired.

'No, Eli, we're heading straight for Canoncito.'

'There's twenty Federal soldiers there, sir,' a worried Whitman reminded Byrnes.

'That's mighty long odds, sir,' Higgins said.

'We don't have a thing to worry about, boys. Kit Geogheghan was my best pal back in New York.'

'With respect, sir,' a doubting Whitman said, 'he wasn't a Union officer then.'

Byrnes smiled. 'That's true, Eli, but that won't make a scrap of difference to Kit.'

Whitman's apprehension increased as they rode openly into Canoncito. Everything there was in chaos. The Union Army had yet to recover from the attack by guerrillas. Byrnes slowed his horse to take a look around. At the far side of a rope corral was a line of wagons that he recognized belonged to the Confederate surgeons. He could see Cora shaking out a blanket, and he raised a hand in greeting. He was about to spur his horse towards her when a Federal sergeant and two privates, all three with rifles levelled, came round the corner of a building.

'Hold it right there, sir,' the sergeant, a hulking fellow with a huge moustache, ordered. 'Forgive me for not saluting you, Captain, but it would seem disrespectful, seeing as how I'm about to kill you.'

'Don't be too hasty, Sergeant,' Byrnes replied. 'I believe Major Geogheghan is in command. Tell him that Captain Roscoe Byrnes is here.'

Totally unimpressed, the sergeant answered, 'I'll give the major your message, Captain, but first I'll be slamming the three of you in the calaboose.'

The three of them were locked in what had the look of a former sheriff's office and gaol combined. Disuse had given the place a foul, musty smell. Before leaving, the sergeant ordered the two soldiers to remain on guard.

'We aren't exactly in a good bargaining position,' Whitman commented sadly.

'We don't have to be,' Byrnes said. 'When Kit hears about this that sergeant will be changing places with us.'

The outer door opened and the sergeant returned with Kit Geogheghan, smartly turned out in the uniform of a major. A smiling Byrnes greeted his old friend.

'Kit, by God it's good to see you.'

'Roscoe,' Geogheghan replied, ignoring the hand Byrnes had put through the bars. 'What brings you here?'

'We've come to collect our medical team, Kit,' Byrnes replied, expecting the door to be unlocked.

Looking coldly at Byrnes, Geogheghan said in a flat tone, 'That won't be possible, Captain. An important battle is imminent and we need those doctors.'

'Do you know what you're saying, Kit? This is me, Ross Byrnes. Surely you haven't forgotten the Bowery

Bastille, Cait, and the good times?'

'I remember,' Geogheghan said dully, 'but that was New York, this is New Mexico, Captain. Past loyalties don't count in war. You men are prisoners now, and I will see that you are treated correctly.' He issued an order to the sergeant. 'Arrange hot food and coffee for the three prisoners, Sergeant.'

'Now, sir?' the sergeant checked.

'Yes, right now,' Geogheghan insisted, and when the sergeant went out he came close to the bars to whisper, 'Listen to me, Ross. I'll do all I can for you. Take this key. After nightfall I'll have a diversion created to call the guards away. There'll be three horses waiting out back for you. Ride like the wind.'

'But, the medical wagons . . .' Byrnes objected.

'I'm turning traitor for you, Ross, risking my life,' Geogheghan hissed. 'Forget what you came here for, just save your own life and the lives of your comrades. Do you promise to ride straight out?'

'I promise,' Byrnes said reluctantly as the sergeant came back in, accompanied by two orderlies carrying steaming mess tins.

The three of them ate morosely as the shadows inside their cage lengthened. When they had finished the meal and were drinking coffee, Whitman asked, 'Do you feel bound to keep your promise to your friend, sir?'

'Like he said, this is war,' was Byrnes' enigmatic reply.

'But there's still only three of us and twenty of them, sir,' Higgins protested. 'We'd be cut down before we got to those wagons.'

'That makes no difference to you two. Take the horses Kit leaves and get out of here.'

'No, sir, I'm with you all the way,' Whitman pledged.

'That goes for me, too,' Higgins was saying, as some muffled sounds came from just outside.

'This is early,' Byrnes exclaimed. It was still twilight.

Then there were some shadowy figures outside the door. Byrnes's name was called as a bearded Symington was peering in at them. Greenham and Strachey stood close behind him.

'What are you doing here, Symington?' Byrnes gasped.

'I got to thinking, as you do sometimes,' Symington began conversationally. 'You could have killed me, but you let me live. So I figure I owe it to you to help get those wagons back.'

'What about Greenham and Strachey?' Byrnes asked.

'They'll do as I say, Byrnes. When you go out you'll step over two dead sentries,' Symington said. 'Just hold on while I send out for something to bust this door open.'

'There's no need. I've got a key,' Byrnes said.

'Well, if that don't beat all!'

A bewildered Symington had barely

finished speaking when the outer door was kicked open and the big sergeant came crashing in. The sergeant lifted his rifle with the intention of felling Strachey, who was nearest to him. Symington's movement in drawing his knife was too quick for Byrnes to catch. But he did see the razor-sharp blade slice the sergeant's throat from ear to ear.

As the sergeant crumpled to the floor, Symington coolly said, 'There's a whole heap of Yankees out there, so we'd better even things up a little.'

He calmly took sticks of dynamite and fuses from a bag he was carrying. Charging the whole front of the building, every stick of explosives linked by a fuse, he trailed a long fuse out through the door and beckoned for the others to follow him.

It was dark now, but in the swaying light of a kerosene lamp hanging outside the gaol, Byrnes saw the bodies of the two sentries lying in the road. Puzzled, he watched Symington go back inside, to re-emerge dragging the corpse of the sergeant and put it close to the sentries. The sergeant's eyes were staring wide, and his moustache had risen at each end in a caricature of a smile. It was as if having his throat cut had amused him.

'That should do it,' Symington said, looking down at the bodies. Throwing his own weapon to Byrnes, he collected the rifles of the two dead sentries and passed them to Whitman and Higgins. 'Right, lads, run to that alleyway across the street. Be ready to start shooting.'

Byrnes went with the others. Symington remained across the street, crouching in the dark beside the gaol, holding the end of the fuse.

Two soldiers came walking along, totally involved in conversation until one noticed the three bodies outside the gaol. They ran to take a closer look, then started shouting to raise the alarm.

More soldiers came running. Taking advantage of the confusion, Symington dashed across the street to report, 'I've lit the fuse, so stand by for the big show, lads.'

The words had hardly left Symington's mouth when a massive explosion rocked and temporarily deafened them. As the dust settled they could see that the gaol was wrecked. Bodies and bits of bodies were scattered around.

A group of five soldiers came rushing up. Knowing they represented the last of Union force at Canoncito, Byrnes took command. 'When I give the order, men, fire.'

The Yankees, devastated by the sight of their dead comrades, came on unsuspecting. When they were close enough to ensure there would be no survivors, Byrnes rapped out the order. The five Union soldiers were blasted off their feet.

'Good work, Symington,' Byrnes complimented the former officer on the scheme that had left Canoncito wide open for them.

'I do what I can,' Symington said

modestly, 'but you take command from here on, Byrnes. What would you have us do?'

'Follow me, all of you,' Byrnes said. 'Our task is to get those wagons back to our army at the Rio Grande before the fight begins.'

They were heading in the direction of the corral when Kit Geogheghan shouted from behind them. 'Captain Byrnes.'

Telling the others to proceed and he would catch up with them, Byrnes walked back. Geogheghan stood about a yard distant from where the men of his command lay dead, holding a revolver waist high.

'I honoured our friendship, Roscoe,' Geogheghan said in a voice shaky with emotion. 'I gave you the chance to ride out of here unharmed, a goodwill gesture that you repaid by ruining me. I am disgraced, finished as an officer, but killing you will make that just a little easier to accept.'

'I am unarmed, Kit. Your men

disarmed us when we arrived.'

Not replying, Geogheghan did a sideways walk towards the bodies, keeping Byrnes covered all the time. Stooping, he reached out gropingly. Finding the holster of a dead lieutenant, he unbuttoned the flap and pulled out a revolver. Straightening up, he returned, crab-fashion and threw the revolver so that it landed at Byrnes's feet.

'Pick it up and use it, Roscoe.'

'No, Kit, this is crazy,' Byrnes protested. 'Man and boy you and me were close friends. Wearing uniforms of different colours doesn't change that. For God's sake, Kit, we spent our lives together.'

'Then with luck we could die together right now. Pick up that gun, Roscoe,' a determined Geogheghan ordered.

With a shake of his head, Byrnes said, 'We have shared too much, have too many memories for us to fight, Kit.'

'You turn away, Roscoe, and as God is my judge, I'll shoot you in the back.'

'I know Kit Geogheghan too well to believe that.'

'Maybe I couldn't have done it before this . . . ' Geogheghan gestured at the shattered, bloodied bodies of his men. 'Be warned, Roscoe: neither you nor I ever knew the Kit Geogheghan who is standing here now.'

'Goodbye, Kit, and may God bless you,' Byrnes said, as he slowly about turned.

Something hit him hard in the back, close to his left shoulder. As he hit the ground, face down, the sound of the blast of a gun caught up with him. The self-preservation instinct instantly kicked in. Twisting his body, Byrnes reached for and found the revolver on the ground. Bringing it up, he fired at his old friend just as the pain of the wound in his back exploded. The agony was too much to bear, and he lost consciousness.

When Byrnes came to he was lying in a hospital tent. His left arm was held securely in a sling and his back was afire with pain. For a moment he thought he was hallucinating when he saw the sweet face of Cora Graycot.

But then she spoke. 'Lie still, Roscoe. You have been badly hurt.'

'Kit Geogheghan?' he asked desperately, but her frown showed that she didn't understand. The sounds of battle came from a distance. 'What has happened, Cora?'

'Thanks to you,' she replied, 'your men got us here in time. I thank the Lord, Roscoe. The battle is going badly for our side, and there are many casualties. We are moving back.'

Byrnes looked round the tent for the first time. Doctors, nurses and orderlies were carrying patients in muddied, bloodied bandages out to waiting wagons. The wounded were being evacuated ahead of a mass retreat by the fighting forces.

'This will be the last battle the Confederate States Army will fight out West, Cora,' he predicted.

'Thank the Lord,' she said fervently,

turning as a dishevelled Eli Whitman and Joe Higgins came hurrying up.

'Good to see you looking better, sir,' Whitman said with a weary smile.

'No doubt I've you to thank for bringing me here,' Byrnes responded. 'What of Kit Geogheghan, Eli?'

Avoiding Byrnes's eyes and his question, Whitman said, 'They've got us on the run, sir. It's a complete rout. We were outnumbered and outfought by the Federals. Symington, Greenham and Strachey went in with the first wave. All three perished, sir. We're heading back to Santa Fe.' He turned quickly to Cora. 'Have you told Captain Byrnes about his father, Nurse?'

Astonished Cora gaped for a moment, exclaiming, 'Oh dear, I should have realized that Colonel Byrnes is your father, Roscoe.'

'What's happened to him?' Byrnes asked, looking anxiously to Cora and Whitman for an answer.

'Colonel Byrnes was badly injured by an enemy shell, sir,' Whitman said in a way that warned Byrnes that his father was either dead or dying.

'He's in the next tent to here, Roscoe,' Cora announced, then regretted it as she tried to keep Byrnes in his bed.

'I have to see him,' he said.

Still wearing his uniform trousers, and with his bloodstained tunic over his shoulders, Byrnes was assisted to the next tent by Whitman and Higgins. They waited respectfully outside as he, dizzy and weak, scanned the shadowy interior for sight of his father. The colonel was in the far corner, and Roscoe made his way to him.

Colonel Rutherford Byrnes seemed to have rapidly aged in readiness for death. He opened his eyes and Roscoe was moved to see a warmth flood into them at the sight of him. For the first time in his life he felt close to his father.

The blankets covering the colonel's chest had been placed over a wooden frame that gave them a squareness. This meant that his father's upper body had been so severely damaged that it couldn't stand the weight of a blanket. Pointing to it, the colonel gave a faint smile and made a joke.

'They've put me half in a coffin already. It's good of you to come to see me, Son.'

'How are you, Father?' Roscoe asked, shocked to realize that he had addressed his father as 'Father' for the first time ever. 'They are moving us back to Santa Fe, so I will arrange for me to be with you as —'

'Hush, Son,' his father interrupted. 'I have things to say. I was wrong to force you into this foolish war, Roscoe, and I pray that one day you may find it possible to forgive me.'

'I have nothing to forgive you for, Father.'

'Hush!' The colonel spoke the word more urgently this time. 'Go home, Roscoe. The war in New Mexico ended this afternoon. We were soundly defeated, Son. You will be repaid in the material sense for the harm I have done to you. Your grandfather assures me that you will inherit all that he possesses. I am also a man of considerable wealth, Roscoe, and you are my sole heir. It is no real recompense, I appreciate that.'

'There is no need — ' Roscoe Byrnes began, but his father wasn't listening. The colonel's head had fallen to one side. He was dead.

Back outside the tent, Byrnes averted his face from Whitman and Higgins. It astonished him to find how deeply affected he was by the death of a man he had hardly known.

Recovering control of himself, Byrnes heard how tight his voice sounded as he asked, 'Tell me about Kit Geogheghan, Eli.'

Whitman was a long time in answering him. Byrnes looked around him at a scene of despair and desolation. More troops were falling back now, some maimed, others with the staring eyes of men whose minds have been numbed by the horrors of warfare. All were ready to help their comrades, and Byrnes watched the competent Cora supervise the loading of stretchers into wagons.

'Major Geogheghan is dead, sir.'

'I killed him?' Byrnes's voice was bleak. He was facing the wrong way to see Whitman's confirming nod, but he had known the answer before asking the question.

'Let us help you back to your tent, sir,' Whitman fussed over him.

'No, leave me for a while, Eli,' Byrnes muttered.

He found the isolation he needed behind a shell-shattered wagon that had been upturned. Byrnes thought of his father, then of Kit Geogheghan. An immense sorrow overwhelmed him. For the first time since he had been a small boy, Roscoe Byrnes wept.

Cora Graycot found him there, head still bowed by grief and guilt. She slipped a comforting arm around his shoulders. They remained silent as the Confederate world disintegrated around them. A change in the tempo of nearby activity had Cora speak gently.

'They are ready to pull out, Roscoe. You are the hero of what has otherwise been a black day. Come, the army will want to reward you.'

'I am no longer a soldier, Cora,' Byrnes disconsolately informed her. 'A new life, a better life, must be waiting somewhere. What I'm trying to find the courage to ask is, will you come with me to find and share that life with me?'

Not answering, Cora looked past the military turmoil to some imagined horizon where the air was not tainted by the stench of war. She took both of his hands in hers, and spoke softly. 'To hear you ask that means everything to me, my dear Roscoe. This is the hardest decision I will ever have to make, and I must not weaken. You are my love, but nursing is my life. There will be other wars, and wherever in the world they may be, I want to be there to help the wounded, comfort the dying.'

With her hand still holding his, they sat for a long while. They didn't speak, for there were no more words ever to be said to each other. Then, still silent, she stood and walked from him. Byrnes watched her go, his heart filled with misery. She didn't once look back.

His unhappiness increased on the way back to Santa Fe, when both Whitman and Higgins, who had something planned together, turned down his suggestion that all three of them share the future.

'I wish you both well,' he said as he shook them by the hand. 'You, Eli, taught me how to be a man.'

'On the contrary, sir,' Whitman replied, 'you have been an inspiration, and always will be.'

'I am privileged to have served under your command, sir,' Higgins, close to tears, told him.

Wanting this to be the final farewell, frightened that their emotions would betray them, the two soldiers moved away from Byrnes. They left him alone, very alone apart from the harrowing company of his ghosts.

Heart weighted by the personal losses he had suffered in so short a time, it was a gloomy Byrnes who reached Santa Fe. Then he heard a joyous shout, and Cait Mackeever came running up to him, laughing and crying at the same time.

'Oh, Ross,' she sobbed, giving him a one-armed hug in consideration of his injured back. 'It's marvellous to see you again.'

He kissed her and, on cue, a brave sun fought its way through a leaden sky to shine on them. Spirits rising fast, he made a decision that filled him with hope for the future. 'Get your things packed, Cait. We're heading back to New York.'

'Oh lovely!' she cried, clapping her hands like an excited child. Then her face went serious as she suggested, 'Let's make it perfect, Ross, by waiting for Kit so that he can come back with us.'

The sun retreated, taking his new-found elation with it. Looking inwardly into the depths of a terrible darkness, he heard his own voice speak from somewhere far off.

'Kit Geogheghan won't be coming back.'

THE END

Other titles in the
Linford Western Library:

THE SAN PEDRO RING

Elliot Conway

US Marshal Luther Killeen is working undercover as a Texan pistolero in Tucson to find proof that the San Pedro Ring, an Arizona trading and freighting business concern, is supplying arms to the bronco Apache in the territory. But the fat is truly in the fire when his real identity is discovered. Clelland Singer, the ruthless boss of the Ring, hires a professional killer, part-Sioux Louis Merlain, to hunt down Luther. Now it is a case of kill or be killed.

TRAIL OF THE CIRCLE STAR

Lee Martin

Finding his cousin, friend, and mentor, Marshal Bob Harrington, hanging dead from a cottonwood tree is a cruel blow for Deputy U.S. Marshal Hank Darringer. He'd like nothing better than to exact a bitter and swift revenge, but as a lawman he knows he must haul the murderers to justice — legally. But seeking justice is tougher than obstructing it in Prospect, Colorado. Hank has to keep one hand on his gun and one eye on his back.